NOT HER BABY

A GRIPPING PSYCHOLOGICAL THRILLER

EMILY SHINER

Cover Design by The Cover Collection

Copy Editing by Rosemary Stewart

Formatting by Emily Shiner

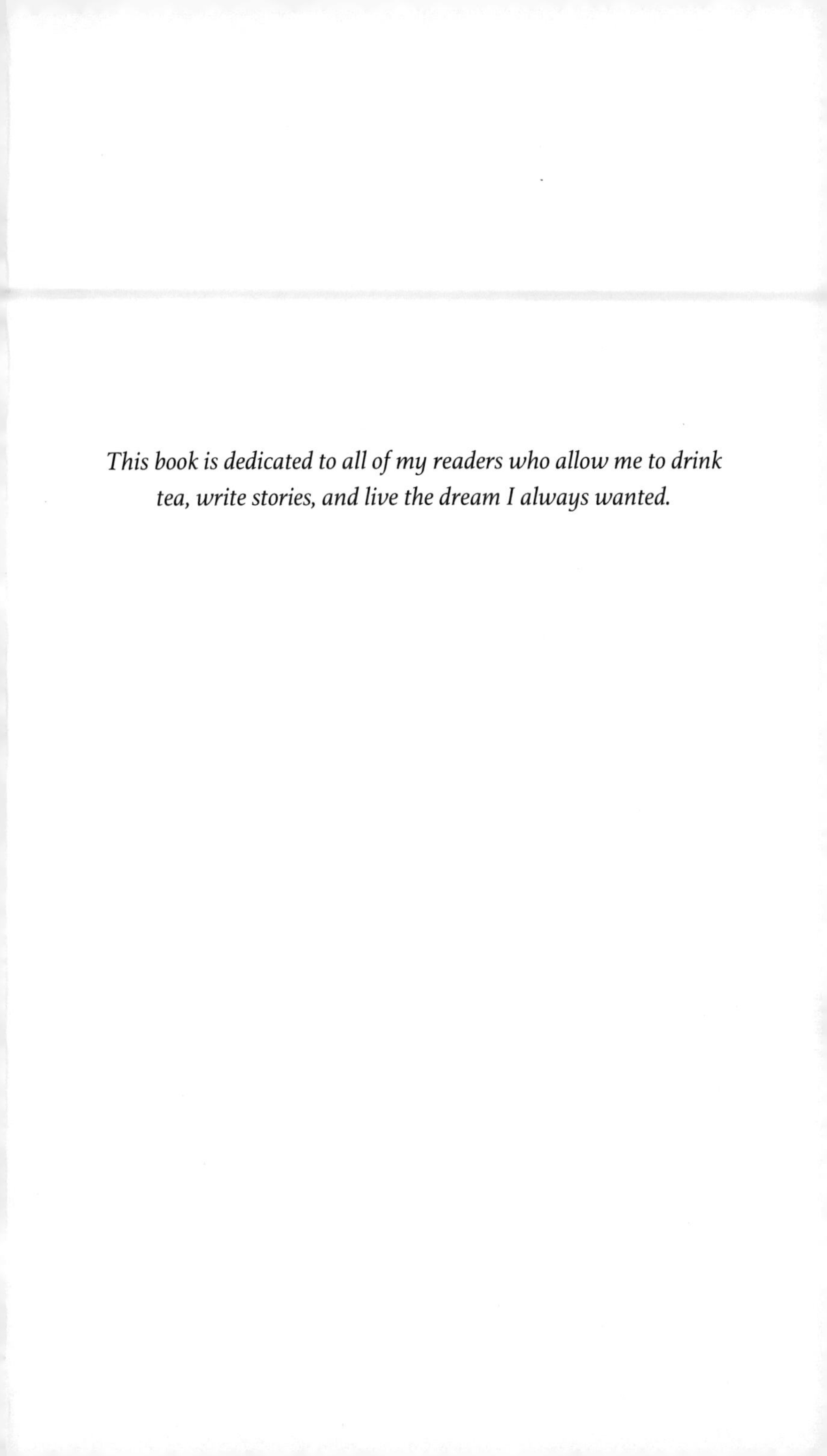

This book is dedicated to all of my readers who allow me to drink tea, write stories, and live the dream I always wanted.

PROLOGUE

The cramping sent me to the bathroom before dinner was over.

My chair scraped against the perfectly smooth wide wood planks in the dining room and I was sure that Alex, my husband, would have something to say to me about that later, but I didn't care at the moment.

The only thing that mattered was getting to the bathroom.

"No, no, no, please," I muttered, locking the door behind me and hurrying to the toilet. For just a moment, I stared at myself in the mirror, but just as quickly, I looked away again.

Staring at myself wasn't going to undo what was happening, and I knew that.

How many times had I been in this exact situation? How many times had I thought that everything was fine, rushed to the bathroom with cramps, and then had to tell Alex that things didn't work out the way we wanted them to?

The way he told me they had to.

I stripped, knowing full well that I was going to make a mess. Another wave of cramps tore through me and I cried out, then bit down on my knuckle, not wanting him to know what I was doing.

He knew, though. I saw the way his face darkened when I got up from dinner, how he silently watched me as I hurried from the dining room. It was the same look I'm sure he gave people at the office.

Like I'd disappointed him.

Like I'd failed him.

Again.

"Why, baby," I whisper, forcing myself to look at the red on my fingers. "Why won't you stay? What do I keep doing wrong?"

Tears sting my eyes but they don't hurt nearly as bad as the cramps shooting through me. They don't hurt nearly as bad as the knowledge that Alex is still at the dinner table, finishing his steak, downing his wine. He won't talk to me about this, won't comfort me, won't hold me to him to try to make things better.

It won't be a discussion, just like it wasn't the last time.

Or the time before that.

The only thing that matters is getting his son, continuing the family line, making sure the Stanfield name doesn't die.

That's my job and, so far, I haven't been very good at it.

All I know is that I better figure out how to make that happen, how to give him his baby, or I don't know what he'll do to me.

1

KATIE

JANUARY

"What are you plans for the day?" Alex's voice is stilted, which is unlike him. When he speaks, he always has his words perfectly picked out so he sounds confident and in control. I complemented him on that once and he told me it was thanks to all the public speaking classes he'd had to take when he was younger.

Up until now, Alex hasn't said much during breakfast, which isn't out of the ordinary for him. Normally he has his laptop open on the table between us and is responding to emails or is reading the news so he isn't — his words — blindsided by any stupidity when he gets into the office.

Today, though, I've had all of his attention, and I'm not sure what to do with it. Even though he's been quiet, he's been watching me, and I can't shake the feeling that he's assessing me.

I don't usually find Alex to be attentive anymore. When we were dating, well, that's a different story. I remember bouquets of flowers sent to my walk-up apartment, him stopping by the café where I worked just to check in on me, him sending me on a shopping spree so I looked the part when he took me out to dinner later that night.

But then things cooled down a little, at least I think they did. After the drama of someone as rich and powerful as Alexander Stanfield marrying a nobody blew over, people really didn't seem to care that he'd found me where I was working in a café, swept me off my feet, and knocked me up before marrying me just a month later.

Sure, there were whispers, and his mother definitely had some things to say to him about *sticking it where it didn't belong* and *besmirching the family name*, but when the ultrasound showed it was a boy, her tune changed.

After his older brother died before having children, everything fell on Alex's shoulders. They all wanted a Stanfield baby to carry on the family name and I was going to be the one to give it to them.

Of course, that baby didn't stick.

We tried again and again, and even though I've talked about adoption as a great option for getting him the baby he wants, that's one thing he and I don't see eye to eye on.

He wants the baby to have Stanfield blood. *I just want a baby.*

"I have that charity luncheon today," I remind him, shifting in my seat. I have a very good feeling I know exactly what he's really asking but that's something I don't want to talk about right now. "Remember, for Hospice? Your family was generous enough to buy a table and I'll be going with your mother."

"Right." He takes a bite of eggs benedict and washes it down with strong black coffee while watching me. He's waiting to see if I'm going to tell him anything else, but I bite my tongue.

Surely he's tired of this monthly song and dance the two

of us go through, right? I know I am — I'm exhausted thinking about if I might be pregnant, debating about when to take a test, wondering whether this month might be the one where I finally do the thing he married me to do.

"And then in the afternoon I'll pick up your dry cleaning, stop by the store to get you some of that whiskey you like, and then I thought I'd roast a chicken for dinner. How does that sound?"

"Steak sounds better. I know you'll make that happen." Another bite of eggs. He chews mechanically, watching me, observing me.

He's trying to tell if I'm pregnant or not.

His eyes flick to my chest, like he'd really be able to tell just from looking at me. Thank goodness he can't see my stomach or I'm sure he'd be examining me for any change. Not like there would be one this early, he's just obsessive when he really wants something.

It's difficult, but I smile at him. "Whatever you want. I'll even make some bearnaise sauce. My last cooking lesson was on different sauces and I can do that now."

He frowns, a furrow appearing between his dark blue eyes. "The egg in that will be cooked, right? I don't want you eating raw eggs."

I flash him a grin and try to tell myself that he's asking that because he really cares about me and wants to make sure I'm safe, not because he's hoping that I'll be pregnant and doesn't want me to do anything that will put the baby at risk.

If there is a baby.

Today's the day I could take a test. I missed my period and while I haven't talked to Alex about it, he knows, just like he knows everything that goes on in this house.

"Oh, the eggs will be fine," I tell him, leaning my chin on

my hand so I can get a better look at him. "You don't have to worry about that, okay? Hopefully we'll have good news today, but you don't have to think about it, I'll let you know as soon as I know anything."

He smiles and, for just a moment, it looks like all of his defenses are down and I see the man I fell in love with when I was working in the café, barely making ends meet. It was like a fairytale, only I didn't believe in love like that when I met him, so I didn't think it could really happen to me.

But Alex was nothing if not persistent. He'd stopped in to grab something on his way to the office because he'd missed the catered lunch he was supposed to be enjoying, but that didn't bother me. It didn't bother me that it was obviously not normal for him to walk into Sunnyside Up Café, where I had been waiting tables for a few months. It didn't bother me that he looked as out of place in my world as I would in his.

It sounds stupid to me now, but he looked at me and smiled, and I'd swear the world slowed down a little bit. There was just something about the expression on his face that made me want to step right into his arms and let him take care of me. Melinda, the girl I'd been working with, had seen the way he'd looked at me while she was seating him and immediately demanded I take her table for her so I could be closer to him.

I was supposed to get off work. I was supposed to eat home and soak my feet and maybe take a nap, but his bright eyes bored into me and I tied my apron tighter around my waist, grabbed the notepad from Melinda, and marched right up to him like I was walking up to my destiny.

And that was it. The rest, as they say, is history. It consisted of amazing dates I didn't think I'd ever experience, spending the night at his incredible home, and then finally, two little pink lines that changed everything in my life in a way I didn't even know was possible.

I love Alex. I know how badly it hurts him that I haven't been able to give him a child yet, and I would do anything to make it happen for us, just like I know he'd do anything to help me out. I can't even count the number of specialists I've been to, the number of medications I've taken, how many shots I've given myself.

He hasn't ruled out IVF, but that's just not something I'm really interested in. If I'm meant to have a baby, I will.

That's what I keep telling myself, at least.

I'm deep in thought when Alex stands, dropping his napkin to the table. I'll clean it all up, just like I always do. He fired his chef shortly after we got married and I've been in charge of all of the cooking. Besides Mary, our maid, we don't have any waitstaff, and that's something that was my decision.

I want a normal life, but it's really hard to have that when your husband is a member of one of the wealthiest families in the south. I could have this house filled with staff, but that's not how I was raised, and it's not the way I want to raise our child, whenever we have one.

"I'm off to work. Katie, come here." Alex motions for me to join him and I do, dutifully standing and walking around the large oval dining room table to step into his arms. He pulls me close and I snuggle right under his chin where I like to stand when we're talking. There's something about being in his arms that makes me feel safer than anywhere else in the world.

Even though I know I'm disappointing him every single month, I know Alex loves me. It's just that sometimes I can't shake the guilt I feel knowing that he married me because I was pregnant.

Because I was already giving him the one thing he wanted so badly.

Sure, he loves me, but I know he'd love me even more if I were able to finally give him the child he wanted so badly.

"I want to know as soon as you take a test," he tells me. His rich cologne wraps around me and I breathe him in, resting my face carefully against his shoulder. His suit is custom, and I don't want to dirty it, but I've gotten better about making sure my makeup won't smear when the two of us hug.

The last thing he wants is to have to change before he goes into the office.

"I'll call you as soon as I know," I tell him. "But I might not have time to take one until you're home. It's going to be a busy day."

He stiffens and I know he really wants me to tell him as soon as I find out if I'm pregnant, but I don't want to promise him I'll take a test this morning.

When I know that peeing on that little stick will very likely ruin my day, why would I rush it?

"We need to make this happen, Katie," Alex says, and his words make me shiver. "The Stanfields need an heir."

2

ALEX

My day was busy, but that's just the way my days are now. I don't know many people who could hack the long hours I spend in the office, the meetings I suffer through, the endless conversations I have with clients to make sure we're on the same page and that they're happy.

It's okay. That's why I get paid the big bucks, why I get the custom car, why I have suits tailor made in the best fabrics. My family has worked hard to become the top investment firm in the south and we didn't do it by clocking out of the office at five, no matter how badly we might want to get home to relax.

Stanfield Investments sits on a huge hill overlooking Main Street. Rather than choosing an office downtown, which would have made us more accessible, my grandfather chose to build his office here, high above everyone. Not only do we get to avoid the smell of hot dogs from a random grill across the street, but our clients can sit out on the second-floor porch, sip on a cool drink and look down at everyone walking around when our meetings are finished. They like that.

Why wouldn't they? It reminds them that they are richer than everyone else in town. I like it, too. There's nothing better than closing a big deal, bringing more money into the company, then sitting out on the porch with a glass of whiskey and watching everyone else scramble about like ants.

We work so you don't have to.

The Stanfield Investments motto is written above the front door and I glance up at it as I walk out to my car. It's been a long day and I haven't heard from Katie yet, which makes me feel a bit edgy. Sure, I heard about the luncheon with my mother and how delicious the caprese salad was, but that's not what I want to hear.

I need to hear that she's finally pregnant. More than that, I need her to be able to carry this baby to term. Everything that my grandfather, father, and I have done has been to ensure that future generations of Stanfields have the life they deserve.

If I don't have a child — a son — to carry on the family name, then what use was any of this? Why should I have put in the long hours? Sure, vacations are great, and having whatever car I want delivered to the house for me to use is wonderful, but we're about building wealth here, building a fucking *legacy*, and I need a son to pass it down to.

My secretary Emma looks up as I walk out and gives me a small wave, but I ignore her. Mentally, I'm already at home. I want to be with Katie, want to hear the good news I've been waiting so long for. How many babies has she lost? Each miscarriage tears her up inside, I know that it does. It can't happen again.

I also know she'd love to adopt, but that simply won't

work for me. I want to keep the wealth I've worked so hard to build in our family without worrying about any birth parents coming to try to take it. No, we have to have our own. I know Katie doesn't agree with me, but she's not the one who's been groomed for this, who's worked her whole life to improve the family business to make sure that our own family is taken care of.

My phone buzzes as I'm getting into my car. Hope surges through me. Katie?

But no. It's just an email from Emma with some questions from a client I met with this morning. Sighing, I click the phone off and slip it into my pocket. The email can wait until tomorrow, or at least until after dinner.

The drive home takes almost no time at all. I'm on autopilot most of the way and I blink when I realize I'm in the garage already. Getting out of the car I stretch, then close the garage door and walk into the kitchen.

It smells good in here. Clean, just how I like it, and it means Mary was working hard today. Over the slightly antiseptic smell, I smell dinner. Slipping out of my jacket and dropping it on the back of the leather sofa in the living room, I walk into the kitchen and loop my arms around Katie, pulling her backwards against my chest.

"Smells good," I murmur, kissing her cheek. "I'm starving, so please tell me the steak is almost done."

She laughs and turns in my arms, kissing me back before pulling away. "Close. I have something delicious prepared, and yes, it's all ready. In fact, it's on the table. Wine?"

I watch as she turns and opens the cupboard above the dishwasher without waiting for my response. She pulls down just the one wine glass and I feel a bit of hope bubble up.

"You're not drinking?"

"White isn't my favorite," she responds, pouring me a glass and handing it over. I take it, my fingers grazing against hers, my eyes narrowing.

"Steak gets red wine," I tell her. We've gone over this. The first time she cooked for my mother she made the mistake of serving steak and white wine together and Morgana Stanfield had been, in her words, simply appalled. The horror on her face was almost enough to make Katie sink down into the floor.

That's when we started the classes. Cooking, baking, hostessing a party. You name it, my wife either knows how to do it by now or will know how to do it by the time I'm finished with her. She may have grown up eating cold Pop-Tarts from the bag in front of the TV for dinner, but that's not who she is now.

Now she's a Stanfield.

"Just trust me," she says, waving her hand in the air like that will brush away my concerns. "Come on, I don't want dinner to get cold. It's under those silver dome things you like to use, but still."

Curious, I follow her into the living room and sit down in my seat across from her. This is an old family table that could easily sit sixteen, but it's usually just the two of us eating together unless we have a dinner party. Soon I'm hoping there will be multiple children around the edges, all of them clamoring for our attention.

"I know you mentioned steak," Katie says, grabbing the handle of her dome and grinning at me like the two of us are in on some big secret together, "but I wanted something else and I think you'll understand why. Go ahead and lift it."

She's absolutely giddy with excitement and I feel a bit of it jump to me as I grip the handle. It's warm from the heat of the food and steam escapes when I lift it and flip it, setting it out of the way. Then my excitement changes to disappointment.

"I didn't want chicken," I tell her, looking up. "What is this?"

"Those," she says, pointing with her fork at my food, "are Cornish hens. You might say they're *baby* chickens. And there are *baby* carrots with a sweet honey glaze."

I stare at her, trying to wrap my mind around what she's saying.

"And buns." She points at some rolls on the edge of my plate. They're sprinkled with sesame seeds and lightly browned. A pat of butter on each one has melted and run down the side to pool on the plate. "Get it? *Buns*? Hot from the *oven*?"

"You're pregnant." I don't even realize that I've hurried around the table until Katie is also on her feet, her arms wrapped around me. "Oh, God, you're pregnant. Katie, this is amazing."

"Yes, I'm pregnant," she chokes out, and I realize she's crying. Tucking her against my chest, I hold her close enough to feel her heart slamming against me hard. "It's happened again, Alex, and I swear to you, I'm going to do whatever it takes to make this one stick, okay? I'll stay in bed all day, I'll eat all the right things, I'll stop running. I don't care what it is, I'll do it. I want this baby with you so very much."

Relief floods through me. "Me too," I tell her, kissing the top of her head.

It's not just that I want this baby. If Stanfield Investments is going to stay in the family and not get auctioned off to the highest bidder now that Father has died, then I need an heir.

It's in his Will. There's some wiggle room, but time is running out.

If Katie and I are going to have any kind of life worth living and aren't going to lose everything then we need a baby, preferably a boy, but definitely one that has Stanfield blood in its veins.

3

KATIE

Two months.

That's how long I've been pregnant, according to the doctor. Clutching an ultrasound in my hand, I walk to the refrigerator and stick it up. It's the first thing that we've ever put on the front of the fridge and I had to stop at the store on the way home from the appointment to pick up some magnets.

Stepping back, I admire the image, then rest my hand lightly on my lower stomach. I'm no bigger than the night I told Alex I was pregnant. I don't look any different, or feel it.

But I threw up yesterday morning after eating some eggs and toast. Alex was thrilled and I'd googled to see if it was a good sign that I was now puking.

Apparently, it was.

Footsteps behind me make me turn and I smile at Mary when she walks into the kitchen. She's older, around my mom's age, and when I asked her once if she was interested in retiring she laughed and told me that she gets paid so well that she probably never will.

"That looks very good up there," she says, crossing her

arms on her chest and leaning against the kitchen counter to admire the ultrasound.

"You think so?" I'm nervous, and I don't know why. Probably because I'm not sure what Alex will say about having something on the fridge. This is the first ultrasound I have of the baby and it looks like nothing more than a dark splotch on the paper. The technician had to point the little bean out to me and assure me that it was really a baby before I'd believe her.

"I think Mr. Stanfield will be thrilled. I know how badly he wants this."

"He does." I step out of the way as Mary opens a cupboard at my feet to get out some fresh towels. "I just hope this one stays put, Mary. I don't know what I'll do if I lose it. Alex almost came apart at the seams the last time."

Clutching the towels to her chest, she watches me, then nods. "I know it's not my place to talk about it, Mrs. Stanfield, but—"

"Katie, *please*," I tell her, interrupting. "You know I want you to call me Katie. Mrs. Stanfield is my mother-in-law, and I hope the two of us are nothing alike."

She chuckles. "You sure are a breath of fresh air, Katie. I'm doing my best, it's just hard for me to call you by your first name. Anyway, I'm sure Mr. Stanfield is over the moon about the baby."

I nod. Yes, I know how badly my husband wants to be a father. I've never met anyone like him: so determined to have a child, but at the same time so unwilling to look into adoption.

"Are you resting?" Mary eyeballs me.

"I am. And taking my prenatal vitamins, and drinking lots of water, and no more getting in the hot tub. I'm doing all the right things."

"Sounds like it. You know, sometimes life just happens and we can only roll with it. You're doing what needs to be done, Katie, and I know you'll get your baby one of these times. Hopefully this time."

"What if I don't?" As soon as the words are out of my mouth, I clap my hand over my lips, wishing I could take them back. They were whispered, but Mary still heard me, I know she did, and she presses her lips together in a firm line like she's trying her best to keep herself from saying something she shouldn't.

"I'm so sorry," I say, reaching out and lightly touching her arm. "That wasn't appropriate at all. Please, just ignore that I said that. Everything's going to be fine. I'm going to have this baby and nothing bad will happen."

"Katie, I like you," Mary says, lightly patting my hand where I'm still grabbing her arm. "You know that I do. I'm here for you, okay? I haven't ever been married myself, but I can only imagine how hard it can be, especially to a man with such high standards. I will do everything I can to support you, and, honestly, you're going to be fine. This baby is going to be fine. You're going to have a beautiful child in seven months and this conversation will be something you barely remember."

"Thank you," I whisper. Before I can say anything else, she gives me a tight smile and turns, hurrying out of the kitchen. I watch her go, then lean against the counter, my legs suddenly feeling weak under me.

It's easy to talk a big game and sound confident, but if I'm being honest, I'm nervous. Sure, we have an ultrasound picture up on the refrigerator, but that doesn't mean anything, does it? And yes, I've made it farther in this pregnancy than I have in any other one except for the first, the one that inspired Alex to put a ring on my finger, but I'm still worried.

Just because there's a baby in there now doesn't mean there will be forever.

"Come on, baby," I say, splaying my hand on my stomach again. "Please, I want you. I love you."

Even as I say the words, I can't shake the terrible feeling that this pregnancy might not last. I don't know what it is, call it a premonition, call it fear, whatever, but there's a part of me convinced that once again the baby won't make it.

And if I'm right, I don't know what I'm going to do.

4

ALEX

The first thing I see when I walk into the kitchen isn't my gorgeous wife, even though she's wearing my favorite apron and standing nervously to the side, holding a drink ready for me and watching my face like she's never seen me before.

It's the piece of paper stuck to the refrigerator.

I walk over to it, hope rising in me when I recognize what it is, and I pluck it from the door, turning to look at Katie, then glancing down at the dark smudge on the paper. "Our baby?"

She nods. "Our baby."

"What did the doctor say?" I set the ultrasound down on the counter and walk to Katie, taking the drink from her and giving her a kiss. "Did everything look okay?"

"Everything was fine." She smiles at me, but the smile doesn't quite reach her eyes. "Baby looks fine, I look fine." She hesitates and I have to take a deep breath to force myself to wait to hear what else she has to say. "The doctor wants me to take it easy because of my history but she said everything looks normal. I'll go back in a few weeks for bloodwork and another ultrasound, but she said there isn't any reason to worry."

"Thank God," I murmur. "I'm so glad to hear it, this really is amazing news." Katie smiles at me but she still looks worried. "What's wrong, do you feel okay? You look pale."

"Just tired. I know I have it better than a lot of women because I don't have to work, but I'm still exhausted. Don't worry, though, I'll have dinner on the table every night when you get home."

"Don't work yourself too hard," I tell her, taking her by the elbow and leading her into the dining room. "If we need to order in a couple of times a week, or hire a chef to help you though the rest of your pregnancy, we can do that. I don't want you to do a single thing to jeopardize this baby."

"I won't." She sits across from me and we lift the domes over our food. My plate is loaded with steak and potatoes, a fresh salad and bread. There's a plate of brownies on the table in between us.

Katie, on the other hand, only has some bread and salad on her plate. She catches the expression on my face and shrugs. "The thought of eating meat makes me want to throw up."

I nod, and we both eat. Even though of course I don't like seeing Katie feeling sick, there's a part of me that's glad she is. Emma at the office told me she threw up almost every day with her first baby and he was healthy. Her second one didn't cause as much morning sickness and she's been a sickly child.

That's not enough hard evidence to prove a connection, but I'm still willing to see my wife stay sick for a few more months if it means we're finally going to have a healthy baby.

"When are you due? Did the doctor say?"

Katie nods and puts her bread down on her plate. She's barely nibbled at the edge of it. "October tenth. A fall baby. So we'll have a sweet little baby before Thanksgiving and Christmas. It'll be amazing to celebrate the holidays with him. Or her—"

I frown. "I'm going to be in Europe then."

"What?" Katie's face falls but she tries to hide it. "Why? When are you going?"

"I'll be there from mid-September through the beginning of November. Stanfield Investments is looking to expand our company overseas and since I'm the face of it, I have to be there."

Katie blinks hard and I can tell she's trying not to cry. "You'll miss the birth..."

It's callous, but I shrug. "Katie, you can do this without me. We'll hire a nanny to help you, we'll do whatever we have to so you have support. This trip isn't optional."

"Neither is this baby, I thought."

"What was that?"

I watch Katie grow pale when she realizes what she just said.

She shakes her head. "Nothing. I'm sorry. It's just that I've been trying so hard and doing whatever I can to have a baby, and now that we're finally pregnant, you're not even going to be here when it's born."

I stand, balling up my napkin and tossing it on the table. It slips off the edge and falls on the floor, but I don't move to pick it up. Katie can get it. Or Mary. I don't care. I just know I need to get out of here, get some fresh air.

"Alex, I'm sorry." Katie stands too, reaching across the table for me. For her to be able to take my hand I'd have to reach for her too, and I don't want to do that right now.

"I'll be in my office," I tell her. "Make sure you rest up so you don't hurt the baby."

She calls for me again but I close the door to the dining room, sagging against it briefly as I sigh, then pushing myself away from the wall and starting down the hall to my office. I know Katie hates how much I work when I get home, but there's always something that needs to be done. Ignoring my email won't work out for me in the long run.

My phone buzzes and I pull it from my pocket, a chill running through my veins when I see what number it's coming from.

Alex we need to talk.

Five words, five simple words that shouldn't make me feel this worried, but the number does. It isn't saved in my phone for a reason. I know starting an affair when Katie was trying so hard to get pregnant was the wrong thing to do, but it still happened.

There are a thousand things I could blame it on. The terribly long hours I've been working. How stressful it is managing more money than anyone should be allowed to have. The way Katie sometimes pushes me away when she's tired and we both know she's not ovulating.

It was anger and resentment, along with frustration, that finally swirled through me in a cocktail I couldn't handle, couldn't keep bottled up.

Well, that was the first time. The second, third . . . those were all on purpose. But I paid her off. I ended things. Can't she understand that?

There's nothing to talk about. You know that things are over.

It only takes a few taps and I've blocked her number. Good.

What I did with her needs to stay in the past. Sure, it was fun. Yes, I enjoyed myself.

But now that Katie is pregnant, I should focus on her. I don't need to be working late and then going out with another woman while my pregnant wife is waiting on me here at home.

Sighing, I slip my phone back into my pocket. I guess I can send her more money if I need to, if that's what she really wants.

I get through a dozen emails that came in while I was driving home and later having dinner with Katie. None of them is terribly important. But that's the thing about dealing with people who have a lot of money: they want immediate responses. They figure that's one thing they pay you for.

I'm about to shut down the computer when I hear the chime of my email again.

"Jesus, people, go to bed."

Instead of closing my computer, which is what I really want to do, I click over to my email tab and open the new message without taking time to check who it's from.

Her.

I almost close the computer just so I don't have to deal with whatever it is she wants, but my hand is acting on autopilot and the cursor moves across the screen to open the email almost like I don't have any control over it.

There's an attachment. No message in the body. Blank subject line.

My mouse hovers over the attachment and I swallow hard before finally making myself click the button to open it.

As soon as I do, my heart lurches.

It's a picture of an ultrasound.

5

KATIE
MARCH

It's been two months since I told Alex that I'm pregnant. I have to say, I really like the change in him. Not only is he around more, he's also more involved, more interested, almost like he cares more than he did before. I'd hoped that would happen when I saw those two pink lines, but it's good to see it playing out that way.

I arch my back and stretch, enjoying the feel of the tension releasing. Alex left for the office an hour ago and now it's just me in the kitchen, slowly picking up breakfast, the sound of classical music on the bluetooth speaker making me feel like I'm in a movie.

This is what I wanted.

I wanted a baby, wanted my husband to dote on me more, and I'm getting it. It's incredible and I do a little dance across the kitchen floor as I make my way to the refrigerator to put the peach jelly away. I bought it from a farm stand at the end of last summer and tucked it away in the cupboard for when we wanted something that tasted like sunshine, and it was perfect on our toast this morning.

Alex took the ultrasound off the refrigerator, but I put it

back up again when his back was turned. He's seen that I put it back up — he has to have — but he hasn't said anything about it and I'm hoping he won't take it down again. It not only makes me happy to see it, but also reminds me of how blessed I am.

Just as I pull the refrigerator door open, I feel a twinge in my abdomen, then a hard pinch. The pain radiates out, washing over me like wave and I gasp, bending over a bit to grab onto myself.

The jar slips from my hand and shatters on the floor.

"No, please, no," I whisper, sinking down. "Be okay, baby, be okay." I'm pleading, lightly tracing my fingers over my belly. "Please. You have to be okay."

Nothing. No movement, no twinges, no cramps. I exhale hard, and just as I'm about to clean up the jelly, a fresh wave of pain rips through my core like a hot knife and I cry out.

I WAKE UP IN BED, the covers pulled right up to my chin and a fan blowing on my face. Blinking, I sit, pushing the covers down so that I can swing my leg out over the side of the bed. Even with the fan going, it's hot in the room, the air thick and heavy.

There's a fine layer of sweat on my upper lip and I wipe it off, groaning as I reach up and lightly trace my fingers along my throbbing forehead.

"What in the world happened?" I wonder out loud, forcing myself to stand. My legs are wobbly and at first I think that it might be better to sit right back down on the bed, but then I steady myself, putting my hand on the mattress, and walk to the bathroom.

I splash water on my cheeks to try to wake up a little,

and it isn't until I look at myself in the mirror that I remember what happened. Then worry and fear circle through me as I rest my hand on my stomach and try to keep myself from crying.

Things had been going so well and then, suddenly, it all came to a crashing halt.

But how in the world did I make it up into my bedroom without help?

My first thought is that Alex is in the house and he helped me to the bedroom, but I don't hear anyone moving downstairs. Fear prickles the back of my mind when I think about how upset he'll be when he learns that something is wrong. If I lost the baby, if something happened to the baby . . . I shake my head, unwilling to think about that.

It's not that I think he would hurt me, but I can only imagine how upset he would be.

"Please be okay," I whisper, lightly touching my stomach. "You have to be okay."

No answer, although it's not like I expected one. I don't feel anything, no baby movement, none of the little bubbles popping in my stomach that I read about online. But there isn't any blood. If there is a baby still alive inside me, the only way to know for sure is to go to the doctor and get an ultrasound.

And I need to do it all without Alex knowing about it.

6

KATIE

I sit on the edge of the bed, my toes curled in the thick rug on the floor, and press the phone hard against my ear as I listen to it ring.

It isn't until someone picks up on the third ring that I exhale hard and realize I've been holding my breath.

"Southeast OB/GYN, this is Beth. How can I help you?"

It still feels like someone has punched me in the gut and I have to force myself to take a deep breath to respond to the woman. I pick distractedly at the edge of the sheet while I speak, my nail running over the crisp white fabric over and over.

"Hi, this is Katie Stanfield. I was hoping I could come in for an ultrasound. I just had really bad cramps and ended up in bed. I'm not sure what happened and I want to make sure that the baby is okay." My tongue feels thick and I have to force the words out.

"Mrs. Stanfield, yes, of course." Gone is the bubbly tone Beth used when she answered the phone. She's all business now. "Can you come in right away? We have an opening in about fifteen minutes. Someone cancelled."

Fifteen minutes. Twisting my wrist, I look down at my watch and my heart sinks when I see it's already 3:30. I'll be cutting it close to get home again before Alex does, but I can always stop somewhere and pick something up for dinner. He'll love that I wanted to get him a surprise.

"I can do that," I confirm, standing back up. My shoes are on the floor and I carefully slip them on while keeping the phone to my ear.

"Great." I hear her typing furiously. "Was there any bleeding, Mrs. Stanfield?"

So much blood.

The words almost leave my lips, but then I realize that I'd be lying. No blood this time.

"None."

"Okay, do you have someone who can drive you?"

The only other person in the house is Mary. Can I ask her to take me to this appointment? Then it hits me that she was probably the person who helped me into bed. Cold fear races up my spine.

What if she guesses there might be something wrong with the baby?

"Mrs. Stanfield? Are you there?"

"Oh, yes, sorry. I just lost my train of thought there for a moment. Baby brain, right?" I give her a small laugh. "No, I'll be driving myself."

She pauses and I'm sure she's going to try to argue with me, so I forge ahead. "See you soon, Beth, thank you so much."

My hands shake as I grip the banister and make my way down the stairs. Once out of the heat of the bedroom, the rest of the house is cool and I'm pleased to see that Mary has some of the windows open to get fresh air into the house while she cleans.

She really is terrific. It took Alex a little while to see that I couldn't balance everything on my own without some help around the house. It was one thing for me to make dinner and keep the house picked up and clean, but to be out in the community as well, showing my face at events all the time to remind people about Stanfield Investments? It was just too much.

Once he saw that I could be just as useful outside of the home as I was in it, he was just fine with me hiring Mary to help.

And boy, does she ever. She moves silently through the house, making sure it's always clean and perfectly picked up. Company could drop in at any time and Alex would not be embarrassed. When she needs cleaning supplies, I buy them, or reimburse her if she does it herself. When she's sick, she takes time off.

Other than that, I don't deal with her very much. The conversation we had about my fear of losing the baby was the most the two of us have ever really talked.

Now I can't help but wonder if she knows what happened.

In the foyer I pause, then walk to the kitchen to grab my purse. I'm half-hoping to see Mary before I go, even though I'm not entirely sure what I would say. She knows that I don't normally nap during the middle of the day. She'd have to know that something was wrong for me to go upstairs and put myself to bed.

If I'm the one who put myself to bed.

I push open the door to the kitchen. Mary turns, a smile on her face, but it fades when she sees me.

"Mrs. Stanfield! Are you okay?"

I don't remind her to call me Katie. Right now there's

only one thing that matters, and it's finding out how much she knows.

"I wasn't feeling great, so I took a nap," I say, watching her face carefully for any change.

Nothing.

Her eyes don't dilate, she doesn't breathe any more deeply than she was. All she does is keep looking at me like she's waiting for me to tell her something more.

"And I wanted to get Alex something special for dinner, so I'm off to do that." Grabbing my purse, I turn, slinging it over my shoulder, and avoiding making eye contact with her.

"You look pale. Do you feel okay? Is it the baby?"

"What?" I turn to stare at her. "Why would you think it might be the baby?"

She's been wiping down the counters and she holds her hands up between us like she's surrendering. "I heard tales from my friends about spending most of the first trimester in bed trying to get the energy to make a sandwich for lunch, never mind running around shopping. Not everyone has such an easy pregnancy, Mrs. Stanfield, that's all."

I feel myself relax and I lean against the counter, grateful for the chance to stand still for a moment.

Maybe Beth was right. Maybe I should have someone drive me to the office to get checked out. I bet if I asked Mary, she'd agree. She's so amicable, so willing to help, and I can't see her refusing to drive me to the doctor if I confided in her, even though that's not part of her job.

But then she'd know what was going on, and she'd know that I'm worried I might be losing the baby.

Again.

As much as I want someone there with me, our cleaning woman probably isn't the best choice. I'd like to think that she would be loyal to me and wouldn't immediately tell Alex that something was wrong, but how can I be sure?

No, I need to go on my own.

"Oh, I'm fine, and so is Baby," I say, smiling at her and resting my hand on my stomach. "I appreciate you asking, but you don't have to worry. If you're ready to leave before I get back, please go ahead and close the windows. I love having them open but the last thing I want is for someone to break in."

Then, before she can say anything else, I sweep out of the kitchen, heading for the garage. She doesn't respond, and I don't expect her to.

I've told her what I want her to do and she's well enough trained to know that she needs to do what I asked. Simple as that.

Still, there's an uncomfortable thought at the back of my mind that Mary might know more than she lets on.

What if she helped me to my bed and I just think I made it on my own?

What if she knows there's something wrong with the baby?

7

ALEX

It isn't unusual for Katie to go to half a dozen stores to find my favorite cheese to pair with crackers for a pre-dinner snack, but it was still a nice treat to come home to.

I've had a lot on my mind.

I sit in my office, enjoying the cheese and crackers and drinking some whiskey while she finishes up dinner. It's a little late tonight, but she said she got tired earlier in the day and took a nap.

That's fine by me. If she needs to stay in bed this entire pregnancy to make sure the baby turns out okay then I'd be willing to tie her to the bedposts myself to make that happen.

Ignoring the fact that I really need to respond to that email I got last night, I make the phone call I've been simultaneously avoiding and looking forward to.

My mother picks up before the first ring has even died away in my ear.

"Alexander, what a lovely surprise. I don't normally hear from you in the middle of the week. Tell me, do you have good news for me ... or is there something that you need?"

I wince, I can't help it. Even though I'm the one in charge of Stanfield Investments, even though I'm the one flying to Europe in a few short months to handle the expansion, even though I'm a grown man, my mother still knows what to say to make me feel terrible.

"Mother, I thought you'd like to be the first to know the good news—" I begin, but before I can say anything else, she cuts me off.

"Katie's pregnant. Well, thank God, I was beginning to wonder if it was going to happen again. Tell me, is she doing everything she can to keep this one?"

I grit my teeth and grip the phone tightly. "She's fine, thank you for your concern. And the baby is, too. Everything here is wonderful and we can't wait to meet the little guy. Or girl."

"Oh, I hope it's a boy. You know that girls only cause trouble. Look at Katie when the two of you met. If she hadn't gone and gotten herself pregnant then you could have married someone who was from a family more like ours."

I ignore the dig. "Anyway, Mother, I just wanted you to know. Of course, we'll keep you updated as we get closer to the due date. I'm sure a baby shower will be in order, and I have a feeling—"

"I'll plan it. She might not be the woman I would have chosen for you, Alexander, especially considering the work we've all put into building the company you now run, but if she can finally give you the baby you need to keep it in the family, then I'll forgive her."

"Thanks. You're all heart."

"I'm coming for lunch this Sunday," she announces. "Please let Katie know that I can't wait to see what she makes but do let her know that I'm eating gluten-free these days. It's the latest thing, you know, and I think I'm a little thinner already."

She hangs up and I stare at my phone before putting it face down on my desk, exhaling deeply. My mother wasn't always insufferable, I'm sure of it, but the longer she's had to wait for a grandchild, the worse she's gotten. Katie's never complained about having to see her at the various charity events they go to, though, and I feel a sudden deep rush of gratitude towards my wife.

Turning on my computer, I glance at the time and navigate to my email, then finish my drink in a long swallow. There's just one loose end I need to wrap up before dinner, one loose end I probably should have handled when I was still at work, but the day just got away from me.

In addition to the email with an attached ultrasound picture that came last night, there's now another, this one without any attachments. It came earlier today, around lunch, but I pointedly ignored it because I was working with clients. Even while discussing investments and returns, though, my mind kept coming back to the unopened message.

The email pops open in front of me. It's short and sweet, just a few lines, but when I read it, anger and fear creep up my spine.

Alex,

I know this may have been a surprise to you, but it shouldn't have been. We both know this is what you wanted. I'm very happy to hear about Katie's pregnancy and hope you have a healthy child in a few short months. If not, you know where to find me — and your other baby.

Jenna

That's it. No threats, no demands of money. Still, I know I need to keep this quiet.

Even though I don't want to respond, I fire back a quick email explaining what I did for her earlier today and reiterating that we're over.

This afternoon I set up an account in her name at a private offshore bank I've dealt with for years and transferred over six figures for her to use however she wants. It's enough to keep her happy for a little while, long enough to buy me some time to figure out how to keep her from ever telling the truth about our child.

The last thing I need is the scandal that would arise if people in town found out that I'd had an illegitimate child while my own wife was struggling to have a baby. People trust me with their money, not only because I'm good at my job, but because I'm a good person.

If this story came out I can just imagine the mass exodus of clients we'd have to deal with. At that point, it might not even matter if Katie and I had produced an heir, I'm sure the business would tank.

Jenna doesn't immediately respond and I click over to the ultrasound picture she sent me. It looks so much like the one Katie put on our refrigerator. They could almost be the same. Squinting at it, though, I see that Jenna is due a month before Katie is.

What if she comes to the house when I'm in Europe? Oh God.

I'm so busy staring at the ultrasound on my screen that I don't notice my office door swinging open and Katie walking up to my desk until she's already leaning over me, her cheek pressed against mine, her eyes locked right on the picture in front of me. The sound of her voice makes me jump.

"That's not mine."

8

KATIE

Alex told me over dinner that his friend's wife is pregnant and they were talking about ultrasounds and that's why he had that picture on his computer. I want to believe him, I really do, but when he told me that, he didn't look me straight in the eye.

But why in the world would my husband lie about something like that? He wants this baby almost more than I do, and there's no reason to think that something is up. Still, he closed the email way too quickly, as soon as he realized I was looking at it. I didn't like that, just like I don't like the strange feeling in the pit of my stomach now.

Add that to the stress of what the doctor told me, and I feel like I'm about to come out of my skin.

The baby is gone.

We did an ultrasound and the little bean, the little black smudge that I'd already been thinking of names for and planning to love for the rest of my life, is gone. It's like it was never there, although my doctor did tell me I'm going to start bleeding soon.

And when I cried and begged her to tell me what had

happened, what I had done wrong, and how I could keep this from happening again, she'd hugged me, shook her head, and told me that these things happen.

These things happen.

She was kind, but she said that matter-of-factly.

I know 'these things happen'. They keep happening to me. I also know how disappointed Alex is going to be when he finds out. I'm already wondering if I can get pregnant again without him learning the truth. I love my husband, I really do, and I know that he wants me pregnant, wants to have a child, maybe even more than I do.

I was so happy about that at first. Having a husband who was over the moon about being a father was the most incredible feeling for me. I knew so many women who had accidentally gotten pregnant and the men they were with weren't supportive. But Alex is different.

That's why I'm not sure I can tell him that the baby is gone.

It's a strange feeling, to decide to lie to your spouse. Never in my life did I think I would lie to Alex about anything, especially something this important, but here I am, already lying by omission by not telling him about my appointment yesterday.

I missed an opportunity to tell him at dinner last night, then another one when we were getting ready for bed. He didn't go back into his office after dinner, which was strange for him, but I rather liked having him around and didn't want to spoil it by telling then. I could have told him at breakfast, but he has a meeting with a big client and kissed my stomach before I left and I didn't want to upset him.

"Oh, hell," I groan, drinking a glass of cold water to try to break out of the funk I'm in. I can't tell anyone what's going on, because I can't trust people to keep their mouths shut around him. Everyone wants to curry favor with Alexander Stanfield, and the only reason I trust my OB not to say anything is thanks to doctor/patient privilege.

Taking a deep breath, I walk down the hall to his office. The door is closed but not locked because Mary has to be able to get in there to clean. He knows that I wouldn't ever go into his office without him around and that I certainly wouldn't ever snoop on his computer.

Not usually, anyway.

But there's something I just have to know.

Now's my chance. He's at work, and Mary is upstairs cleaning our bathroom. Still, I pause in the hallway, listening to make sure she's not coming down the stairs. When I don't hear footsteps, I let myself into Alex's office, quickly closing the door behind me.

I need to know about that ultrasound.

Alex told me it's from a friend whose wife is pregnant, but he was clearly in shock while he was looking at the computer screen. As much as I don't want to believe that my husband would lie to me, isn't that exactly what I'm doing to him?

His leather chair sighs a little when I sink into it and I have to resist the temptation to adjust its height. I won't be here long, just long enough to quickly look at that email, and then I'll leave. I can't let Mary see me in here on the off chance she'd say something to Alex, and I certainly can't make any small changes to his desk that would clue him in that someone was in here moving things around.

His screen turns on immediately and I hesitate, my hand on the mouse.

"You have to know," I say, and hold my breath as I open his email. I know I was emotional last night and definitely under a lot of stress after the doctor's appointment, but there's no way I made this up, right?

Tears sting my eyes and I angrily wipe them away, opening his inbox to find the email.

It's not there.

I have to wade through dozens of emails that have already come in this morning and I flick past them, my finger hitting the scroll button on the mouse.

"No," I whisper, after I look through a week's worth of emails. "I just missed it, that's all. It's here somewhere."

I work my way through them slower now, really taking my time, checking every email with an attachment. Unfortunately, Alex gets emails with attachments all day long and I want to move slowly to make sure I don't miss it a second time.

"It has to be here," I mutter, sitting back in the chair. There's a fine sheen of sweat on my forehead but I don't move to wipe it off. I know I'm on borrowed time and that Mary could come downstairs at any moment. Even if she didn't want to come into Alex's office to clean, she might be looking for me.

She's been checking in on me a lot since my nap yesterday. I know I still need to ask her if she's the one who put me in bed but I don't want to admit to myself that she might know what's going on.

"His trash," I say, clicking on the trash folder. Nothing. I sit back in despair, ready to shut the entire thing down.

Then there's a soft *ding* and a notification pops up that he's gotten a new email.

My hands shaking, I click back to his inbox.

Jenna.

I swear, that's the name I saw on the email last night. Whoever Jenna is, that's who sent Alex a picture of an ultrasound and now she's emailing him again. I'm about to click on the email when I stop myself.

Alex hasn't opened it yet. Knowing my husband, he's probably got his email open on his work computer and is well aware that the email has come in. Strange that he hasn't opened it yet. Maybe he's with a client, or on the phone.

Or maybe he just doesn't want to deal it and he's ignoring it for now. If that's the case, it might take him a long time to open it. All I know is that I can't open it without him doing it first, because he'll notice.

He'll notice and then he'll want to know what I was doing on his computer. If I tell him I'm curious about Jenna then he might lie again, like I'm sure he did yesterday.

Pulling my phone from my pocket, I fire off a quick text to him.

Miss you. How's work?

I'm not really expecting an immediate response, especially if he's in a meeting, but I get one before I have a chance to put my phone down on his desk.

Boring. Just in my office getting ready for a meeting later. You feeling okay?

If he's in his office, I'm sure he's seen this email. I respond that I'm fine, just going to rest for a bit, then jump when the computer dings again.

Another email, this time from someone else.

This one is clicked on almost immediately and the font in the subject line changes from being bold to not.

He's reading his email right now. Alex is at his desk, going through his email. He has to know he has received this one from Jenna, he just doesn't want to look at it. He doesn't want to see it.

Why not?

I'm so tempted just to open it and then mark it as unread

as quickly as possible. Maybe he wouldn't even notice. Maybe he's so engrossed in whatever the other email is that he'll never see that I've read the one from Jenna.

Before I can do anything, though, there's a knock on the office door. Jumping, I half-rise, then sit back down, panic washing over me.

"Katie, are you in there?" Mary sounds concerned.

My eyes are riveted to the door, waiting to see if she's going to let herself in. She doesn't. The handle doesn't turn, but it might, and then she'll see me sitting here and wonder what in the world I'm doing.

I have to close his email so I can tell her I'm just looking for something in his desk drawer — medical insurance stuff maybe? That would make sense. Dragging my eyes from the door to the screen, I navigate to the corner of his email to hit the X and then pause.

The email from Jenna has been deleted.

9

KATIE

I sit and stare at the screen for a moment, but then Mary knocks again. I click the X, close the laptop, and stand, moving away from the chair and pushing it back in place before crossing the office to reach the door.

The handle turns as I reach for it and Mary pushes the door open. "Oh, you're in here! Are you okay? I've been looking everywhere for you because I was worried after yesterday."

"I'm fine," I say, hoping to gloss over what she just said, but I heard it and I'm sure she meant for me to. "Not taking another nap like yesterday. Thanks for checking on me."

She glances over my shoulder. From here she can easily see the laptop and I'm grateful I managed to close Alex's email and get the whole thing shut down.

"No more passing out?"

"Hmm?" I'm halfway out the door, trying to get past her before she can stop me, but her question makes me turn to look at her. "What did you just say?" Fear eats at me. I know that it was silly of me to think — or hope — that she didn't know that I'd passed out in the kitchen, but to hear her mention it like this now, so calmly, is enough to make me feel sick.

Mary smiles and there's something about it that gives me chills. "No more passing out. I found you in the kitchen yesterday and I helped you up to your bedroom. Don't you remember?"

Slowly, I shake my head. The question I want to ask her is in my mouth, but I'm afraid to ask it.

But I don't have to. Mary clearly doesn't have the same qualms about speaking up that I do.

"You seemed pretty out of it, poor thing, but begged me not to tell Alex."

Oh, shit.

Sweat breaks out on my brow and it suddenly feels like the air in the house is so tight, so close and heavy, that it might choke me. It's like falling into the lake with jeans on, the clammy feeling of the heavy fabric clinging to you and making it almost impossible for you to kick your legs to swim.

"I need air," I say, finally pushing past her into the hall. She's behind me as I throw open the back doors and step out onto the deck. It's a gorgeous day, with just enough of a breeze to dry the sweat on my face. I turn my head to it, gasping for air.

"Katie, what's wrong?" Mary's at my side now, her hand on my shoulder, her face etched with concern. "You were so sick yesterday and you didn't want me to tell Alex."

"But did you?" I look at her sharply, suddenly afraid that she might have ruined it all and told Alex that something was wrong. If he guessed that I felt the cramping, guessed that the baby was gone . . . I don't know what he would do.

If he hears it at all, it sure as hell can't be from our maid.

"Tell him?" She shakes her head. "No, of course not, you

really didn't want me to. You didn't want me to call the doctor, either. What happened? It was difficult to make out exactly what you were saying. Your words were slurred."

Maybe she doesn't suspect.

I can blame passing out on just being lightheaded, blame it on not eating enough because I get sick when I do. Nobody would think twice about it, and I might be able to keep up this charade a little while longer.

But then what? Eventually it's going to be obvious that I'm not really pregnant and when that time comes, I can't imagine what Alex will say or do.

He'll be devastated. I know he's told his mother. Everyone at his work knows, and he's over the moon.

I'm supposed to be just as happy as he is. I'm supposed to be working on a nursery and thinking about baby names.

As much as I'd like to do that, there just isn't any baby to plan for, and I think Mary knows that. She knows I don't need to get paint to paint the nursery. That I don't need to choose a rocker and a crib. That any baby shower hosted for me is going to be a farce.

It's in the way she's looking at me, like she can see right through me and I hate it, hate how she's looking at me, hate how empty and broken and lost I feel.

It's not just because the baby is gone. It's because I know that's how upset Alex will be when he finds out. And it's also because someone else is sending him pictures of an ultrasound and he's clearly hiding them from me by deleting the emails and — *oh God is the baby his*?

"Katie, you were saying something about losing the baby," Mary tells me, and her voice is so calm and so kind that I stare at her, my heart slamming in my chest, doing my best to keep from passing out but knowing full well that I'm about to keel over. My knees are weak and she must see it in my face because she reaches out and grabs me, looping her arm around my waist. "You're okay, Katie," she says, murmuring the words at me like I'm a small child. "You're going to be okay."

I want to shake my head and tell her that I'm not going to be okay, that she doesn't understand, but she's already leading me over to some of the chairs we have set up on the deck. I sink into one gratefully, the soft cushion forming itself to my body so I can relax.

Except I can't.

"I'm sorry if I was babbling. What exactly did I say?" I ask, trying to keep my voice casual. "Was it bad?"

For a moment, she doesn't answer, but then she shakes her head and smiles at me.

Some of the tension in my body releases.

"It wasn't bad, Katie," she tells me, flashing me perfectly white teeth. "You were just so worried about the baby, but that makes sense, doesn't it? I mean, can you imagine how heartbroken Alex would be if you lost the little bean? He'd be crushed. You were just worried, that's all."

I nod, but there's a part of me that doesn't quite believe her. I don't know what it is, maybe the way her head is tilted as she watches me, maybe it's the way her tongue darts out and runs against her lip.

Whatever it is, there's a tightness in my chest that I can't shake.

"My throat is so dry," I say, trying to regain control of the conversation. "Do you mind getting me something to drink? I'm parched."

"Of course." Mary's face changes a little, like a mask drops down over it, and before I can get a better look at her, she's walked past me into the house.

I don't relax until I hear the door shut behind her, then I drop my head into my hands, taking deep breaths.

I need to tell Alex about losing the baby.

He'll be angry and heartbroken, but he might do something more. He's told me again and again that he has to have someone to carry on the family name.

Why it's so important to him, I'm not sure, but it's obvious that having a child with him isn't optional. He's made it abundantly clear that if we're going to stay happily married I need to make him a father.

Now I have another fear to add to the worry that I might not be able to do that for him.

What if someone else already has?

10

ALEX

Jenna doesn't want to go away, doesn't want to hear that I'm not interested in the baby she claims is mine, doesn't want to believe that now all of my attention is on Katie.

Where it should be. Katie is my wife. Jenna is not.

As much as I'd like to think that it isn't, Jenna's baby is probably mine, even though I was so careful when I was with her. Or I thought I was.

Maybe, subconsciously, I wanted this to happen. I try to remember if I used a condom the last time we were together a few months ago, and I can't.

It doesn't matter now.

Shaking my head to clear it, I look over at the passenger seat and the gift bag of goodies I had my secretary pick up for me. Emma had been thrilled to be handed the company credit card and told to go baby shopping, and I have to admit she did a good job.

Much better than I would have.

My phone buzzes when I get out of the car but I ignore the notification, focused more on getting into the house and seeing Katie. I want to be there for her right now, especially since as I'm going to be leaving in a few months.

Traveling, even for work, has never been a chore for me. I love it, love seeing new places and meeting new people, but now knowing that Katie will have our baby while I'm gone, I almost wish I could stay behind with her.

It's not that I could really prevent anything bad from happening, but I want to keep an eye on her, make sure she and the baby make it through this okay. I really need that heir.

"Alex!" Katie hugs me as I step through the door into the house, wrapping her arms around me and giving me a kiss. "You're right on time and I hope you're hungry. I made burrito bowls and margaritas. Yours has the good stuff, mine is virgin. Of course."

"Of course," I say, kissing her back and trying to forget about the thoughts I was just having. "Here, I brought you something."

I press the gift bag into her hand and she gasps in surprise, as if she didn't see me carrying it when I walked into the house. "Alex, thank you! Can I open it now?"

"Please do." Following her into the kitchen, I hang my jacket up in the hall closet and glance at my phone before turning the ringer to silent. It was Jenna, just like I knew it would be. Dammit. I sent her money, showed her that I was willing to take care of her and our baby, but I also tried to make it very clear that I don't want a relationship with her.

But she's persistent.

"Oh, Alex," Katie says, pulling cute onesie after cute onesie out of the bag and laying them out on the counter. She runs her hands over each one, smoothing out the fabric. "These are darling — oh, what's this?"

My heart lurches as she pulls out one final box, small,

from the bottom of the bag. I knew I should have gone through the bag before bringing it home but I really didn't have time to do that. I trusted Emma to pick out something good for her and now I'm wondering what in the world she bought.

"Open it," I say, lightly resting my hand on Katie's lower back so I can look over her shoulder. "I can't wait for you to see it."

She hesitates, then her fingers shake a little as she lifts the lid and finally looks inside. A gasp, so soft I can barely hear it, leaves her lips.

I stare into the box.

Emma deserves a raise.

A fine silver chain is wrapped around itself in the box, but it's not the chain both Katie and I are staring at, no matter how pretty it is. There's a small charm on the chain that says "mom", a diamond tucked right in the middle of the O, the letters perfectly swirled and feminine, the entire thing gorgeous.

"Oh, Alex, I love it," Katie says, and when she turns to me, she has tears streaming down her cheeks. "Where did you — no, I don't want to know. I don't care where you got it, I'm just thrilled that you did. Seriously, this is amazing. Wow. I never expected anything like this."

I didn't, either.

"Let's put it on you," I say, taking the box from her and pulling out the necklace. Katie dutifully turns, gathering her hair into a ponytail and lifting it off her neck so I can put the necklace on her. The clasp is fine and small and it takes me a minute of fiddling to get it done up. "There you go," I murmur, taking her by the shoulders so I can turn her and look at her. "That looks amazing. It's perfect, just like you."

"I love you." Leaning against my chest, Katie hugs me

again. "You have no idea how wonderful this makes me feel. It's like you knew exactly what I needed to feel a little better about everything."

"Whoa, what do you mean, baby?" Pushing her away, I search her face for answers, but she turns and hands me a margarita, grabbing another glass for herself and clinking the two of them together. "Are you okay?"

Katie laughs, but the sound is hollow. Stress?

"I'm fine, I'm fine. I'm sorry, I didn't mean to make you worry. It's just that being pregnant is harder than I thought and I'm tired all the time but it doesn't matter, I love it! I seriously would do this every single day for years if it meant the two of us would have a child together."

"Cheers to that," I say, taking a sip of my margarita. It's stronger than she usually makes them and I pause before taking another sip. "I have to say, honey, pregnancy makes you glow. I might just have to keep you knocked up for a while until we have an entire football team running around here."

Her face falls for a moment, at least I think it does, but I'm taking another sip and I might be wrong.

"How about soccer," she says, turning away from me to put our food in bowls. "The brain damage that comes with playing football isn't worth it. I'll make us a soccer team, though."

"This is why you're an amazing mom already," I tell her, taking our drinks to the table in the other room. At the door I pause, looking back at her to make sure she hears me. "You'll do anything for this baby, and it's not even here yet."

She doesn't answer, probably because she's so busy putting together our meals. That's one thing I've always liked about Katie. She's easy to read.

There are other women in my life who make it difficult

for me to tell what they're thinking, but Katie isn't like that. What you see is what you get with her.

The door to the kitchen closes behind me and I put the drinks down on the table, pulling my phone from my pocket before I can stop myself.

Just the one email from Jenna. My finger hovers over it. I have to know what she wants. I thought I made it very clear that whatever there was between us is over now that Katie is pregnant. Maybe things would be different if my wife couldn't get pregnant. Maybe things would be different if my wife lost this baby.

I need an heir.

Tapping the screen, I barely have time to glance at the email that pops up when the door to the kitchen swings open and Katie walks through, carrying our meals, her eyes locked on my face before they flick down to the phone in my hand.

11

KATIE

MAY

It's been two months since Alex gave me the *Mom* necklace.

Two months since he told me he knew I'd do anything for the baby, even though it wasn't even here yet.

Two months that I've been trying to convince myself that he doesn't have another child on the way with a woman named Jenna.

Two months since I lost the baby.

Fingering the necklace, I stare at myself in the mirror, turning to the side and running my hand over my completely flat stomach. It's not that I should be huge by now, but some kind of change would be a great way to convince myself and other people that I'm pregnant.

I know I should just come clean with Alex. I know I should tell him the truth before this spirals out of control, but I feel like that's already happened, and it's too late now.

Besides, I overheard the conversation he had with his mother last night. I didn't have to hear her side of it to know that telling Alex that I'm no longer pregnant with his child would be the worst thing I could do right now.

I'd been on my way to bed, so sleepy that I felt like I was walking through a dream. I don't hum, ever, but still there was a tune coming from my lips.

A lullaby.

I thought I'd just poke my head into Alex's office, tell him goodnight, and ask when he was going to come to bed. He used to come up after me, but since I'd gotten pregnant, he'd been more attentive, looping his arm around my waist to pull me close as he helped me up the stairs, whispering into my ear about how much he loved me, resting his hand on my stomach.

His office door had been open a crack and I'd reached out, my fingers lightly touching the thick wood before I heard his voice, hard and harsh, filled with anger and frustration, and I'd caught myself back at the last moment. My hand stayed on the door but I didn't push it open, didn't move or make a sound to let him know that I was standing there.

I didn't have to strain my ears to hear what he was saying. If he'd realized that his door was open, even just a crack, I'm sure he would have been more careful about what he was saying and how loud he was about it, but as it was it was as if I was standing in the room with him, his words washing over me.

No, not washing over me. They were sliding down my throat, choking me, like thick brackish water, so terrible that I wanted to peel off my skin and scrub myself clean.

"I know perfectly well what will happen if she doesn't have this baby. You think I don't? Everything I've ever done has been to make sure she keeps the damned thing."

There was a warning note in his voice, a low growl I didn't think I'd ever heard before. Goosebumps broke out on my skin, popping up all over my arms and legs as well as the back of my neck.

Silence, then he spoke again. "She's *gone* to doctors, Mother. She's doing everything she can to get pregnant and stay that way. Believe me, I know how important this is. I'm not going to risk losing the company just because she can't have a child, and I'm willing to do whatever it takes to have one with my name attached to it. I want it to be Katie's, but if it has to be someone else, so be it. I see that, don't worry."

My head had begun to spin. He was going to lose the company if he doesn't have a baby? Worse, he was willing to have a baby with anyone who could give him one? I knew I should walk away, should go to bed and rest, should wait for things to make more sense in the morning, but my feet were rooted to the floor and I couldn't move.

It felt like an hour that I stood there, my legs growing more and more tired as I forced myself to keep from moving even an inch, then suddenly he was finishing up the call. *Shit.*

I carefully stepped away from the door. A floorboard creaked and even though I knew it was stupid, even though I knew I should just talk to him when he came out of his office, I hurried away down the hall, the words he'd said so painful I couldn't understand them.

Now I stare at myself in the mirror, trying to make better sense of what I heard last night. Alex had come to bed late, much later than usual, and he didn't wrap his arm around me like he normally did.

"He knows," I whisper to myself, tracing my finger along my collarbone and then lifting up my shirt to look at my flat stomach taunting me. "He knows you were listening, knows you heard it all."

My heartbeat slows and I drop my shirt. No matter what

I heard last night, I can't let him know that I did. It's imperative that I keep him in the dark, that I don't let him know that I'm onto him.

Not only will he lose the company if he doesn't have a child, but it sounds like he's happy to have one with someone else.

Jenna.

My stomach twists and even though I haven't had anything to eat this morning, I rush to the toilet, flip up the lid and grab the edges, shoving my face down into the bowl as everything I ate last night comes back up. My fingers cramp from holding onto the toilet but I don't let go.

The hard tile hurts my kneecaps but I stay where I am, breathing heavily, water and vomit dripping from my lips.

"Katie." Alex is there, right behind me. "Katie, sweetie, let me get you a towel."

He runs the tap to wet a face towel and then takes me by the shoulders, gently pulling me to my feet. I feel uneven, shaky, and even though I don't really want to lean on him for support right now, that's exactly what I do.

I hadn't realized he was in the bedroom, hadn't realized he was going to hear me throw up, but maybe it's for the best.

"Morning sickness," I murmur, letting him wipe my face. The damp towel is cool and the water feels good on my skin. "I keep thinking I'm over it but then it rears its ugly head again."

"I hate that you're sick so often, but like we talked about, it's a good sign. Throwing up means there's plenty of hormones running through your body from growing a baby." Hugging me, he tosses the towel into the sink.

I let him hug me even though I know this is the perfect time to come clean about everything, but how can I? How in the world can I look at this man I love so much, the man I swore I'd be faithful to for the rest of my life no matter what happened, and tell him the truth?

By not telling him I'm lying, but then again so is he.

I guess the only thing that matters is who can keep their secret longer.

12

ALEX

"Are you sure you don't want me to stick around, just to make sure everything runs smoothly?" I'm playing the role of a dutiful, caring husband when I ask Katie this question. I'm sure she can see right through me and knows that sticking around during her baby shower is the last thing in the world I want to do.

Why would I want to hang out as a flock of women descend on the property, all of them dressed to the nines, bearing gifts, and ready to eat dainty finger food while playing ridiculous games?

I wouldn't, and she knows it. I'd much rather go to the bar, or to the office, or do most anything else in the world. I don't need to sit here while my wife opens gifts and oohs and ahhs over all of the expensive baby crap people have bought us.

I don't care about any it. Not the bouncers, rattles, bottles, onesies, or toys. I just care about the baby having my blood running through its veins so I can make sure I keep the company and Katie and I aren't suddenly destitute.

I've thought many times that I should come clean with

her about why I want a child so badly and why I'm not willing to adopt, but nothing good could come from that. She'd get angry with me and cause a scene, and that kind of stress could put her pregnancy at risk.

Still, I watch her as I pull back from her. Her eyes are locked on mine like we're both searching each other's faces for some truth that we're trying to keep hidden.

What secret could my wife be keeping from me?

"We're going to be just fine without you here, don't you worry," she tells me, leaning up to kiss me. Her hand is on her stomach, like it so often is these days. "Besides, the fun part comes once baby is born."

"Oliver. Or Anna," I say, trying out the names the two of us have come up with. "Both of them are good names and I really don't care if we have a boy or a girl. All that matters to me is that they're healthy."

"And me," Katie says, tilting her head to the side a little bit as she looks at me. "I'd like to be healthy, too."

"That, my dear, is a given," I say, kissing her. When she leans into me, I fork my hand through her hair to hold her in place.

But the baby matters more.

"Glad to hear it." A smile plays on her lips and she steps back, flapping her hand at me. "Now, shoo. No offence, you're just going to be in the way here today. It's a girl party, unless this is Oliver in here, of course."

"Of course." I watch her for another moment, then pat my pockets to make sure I have everything: phone, wallet, keys. "Don't have too much fun, okay? I want you feeling your best through the rest of the pregnancy."

"You're amazing. More men should care the way you do," she tells me, and I wave at her as I turn to leave.

The kitchen is already full of a gaggle of women

bumping into each other as they put together food. Mary flits through them all effortlessly, pointing and adjusting, getting people the good silver when they ask, making sure nothing gets broken. I watch as she hands my mother a serving platter before turning and helping someone get a pitcher out of a high cupboard.

She's got everything under control.

As difficult as it is for me to let someone else handle things when I want to be in charge, I leave the house and get into my car. My bluetooth connects to my phone right away and I turn on some music before backing out and heading towards town.

Katie didn't ask what I was going to be doing today during her baby shower, and I didn't say.

It's best if she just comes up with some idea on her own, if she thinks I'm going to the office or maybe picking up a baby gift for her.

If she knew the truth, if she had even an inkling that I was going to go spend time with the mother of my other child, there's no way in hell she'd ever let me out of the house.

13

KATIE

I've barely taken a bite out of the cake on my plate.

The frosting is thick, sugary and cloying. It coated my tongue on the first bite I had of it and I wanted to throw up.

Of course, what better time to throw up? Every woman here would feel sympathy for me and think that it was because of the baby, not because the cake was gross, but that couldn't be farther from the truth.

There's no baby.

There's no baby.

There's no baby.

The three words run through my head like a mocking singsong refrain that I can't get rid of. They play as a background to the rest of my day, constantly running through my mind, always on the verge of my lips like they're going to spill out of me.

That would be the stupidest thing I could do. I keep my lips pressed tightly shut around Alex and his mother. The last thing I want is for either of them to figure out what happened.

And yet — why? It's utterly insane of me to pretend that I'm still pregnant when I'm not, and I know I need to come clean with Alex and let him know that I lost the baby, that I'm sorry. But how in the world am I supposed to do that after what I heard last night?

He doesn't just want a baby. He *needs* a baby.

A hot flush creeps up my chest and I grab the bottle of water next to me, crack it open, and take a swig. It's cool, but not cold enough, and I want to get up and pour it into a glass with ice. I'm half-rising from my seat, doing my best to ignore the way everyone in the room is looking at me when my mother-in-law reaches out and grabs my arm.

"Where are you going, Katie? You don't want to miss out on any of your celebration!" Her words are kind but I see the glint in her eyes telling me that I need to sit back down before I ruin this.

"I just want some ice," I say, holding up the bottle of water. "It's not cold enough."

"That's why you have help," she says, snapping her fingers in the air to get Mary's attention, then grabbing the bottle from me and holding it out to her. "My daughter-in-law can't drink warm water, Mary. Get her something cool, why don't you?"

Taking the bottle, Mary gives me a nod, then she turns and disappears into the kitchen.

"I don't mind getting it," I say, but Morgana just shakes her head like she's really disappointed in me. "If you give the help an inch, they'll take a mile. You have to make sure they know they're here to serve you, not the other way around. Especially with a baby coming."

"I guess you're right," I tell her, meekly settling back in my seat. I'm surrounded by opened gift bags, plates of half-eaten food on the table, and women who are all talking and laughing. Some of them have glasses of champagne and just looking at them makes my mouth water.

I can only imagine how Morgana would react if I were to take a sip of alcohol.

"You need to eat something," Morgana announces, standing and getting me a plate with some fruit and cheese on it. "I don't think you've gained an ounce since Alex called with the good news."

Out of the corner of my eye I look up to see Mary standing in front of us. She has a small smile on her face, almost a smirk, and her eyes are wide, like she can't believe what she just heard.

"Your water, Mrs. Sanderson," Mary says, her eyes locked on mine.

My mouth is suddenly parched and I reach out to take it from her, doing my best to keep my fingers from brushing up against hers. I don't know what it is, but there's something in the expression on her face that makes me nervous.

She heard the comment Morgana just made about me not gaining weight, didn't she? It's obvious she did by the way she's looking at me, like she's just waiting to hear what I'm going to say in response.

And she was the one who helped me get to bed when I passed out. "I need to pee," I say, standing and shoving the water back into Mary's hand. "Excuse me."

My stomach churns as I hurry from the room. I feel lightheaded, like I'm going to pass out, and I stumble in the hall, careening into the wall. I start to black out and I close my eyes, leaning my forehead against the wall.

Then the cramps come.

"Oh, God," I moan, my hand fluttering down to my stomach. "No, no, not right now."

My periods have always been painful, have always come

on out of nowhere, knocking my feet out from under me and making it difficult for me to breathe. So this is nothing new, but it's really not the right time.

"Not right now, *please*," I mutter. I'm wobbly, my knees feel like they're going to give out, and there's a terrible wrenching feeling in my stomach that makes me feel like I'm going to throw up. Digging the fingers of my right hand into my left palm, I take a step down the hall, breathing through my nose, doing everything I can to stay conscious.

The last thing I need is for someone to find me here in the hallway, passed out, bleeding, obviously not pregnant.

I know I need to end this charade. I know I need to come clean with everyone and stop the lie. But now that I'm this deep into it, I'm not sure how I can do that. I have no idea how in the world I'm supposed to look Alex in the eyes after all this time and tell him that I'm not really pregnant.

And what about his mother? And the business?

Stumbling down the hall, I throw open the first door on the right and step into the guest bathroom. The lock on the door is broken, has been for years, but Alex and I have never worried about getting it taken care of.

Why would anyone really need to lock this bathroom door? It didn't seem like something that would ever be a problem.

Until now.

"Shit," I mutter, turning on the light and the fan and yanking down my pants.

There's blood. Lots of it.

Way more than I expected. Even more than when I lost the baby.

It's bright red, almost shiny in my underwear, mocking me, telling me that this is all my fault.

Throwing open the cupboard under the sink, I grab a

towel and frantically try to wipe the blood off my legs. My periods are heavy, but this is ridiculous.

This is like something out of a horror movie.

Bending over, I dig around under the sink, desperate to find a pad, some extra underwear I might have stashed in there on a whim, anything.

My back is to the door so I don't see it open, but I hear it.

The voice, when the person speaks, is breathless.

"I knew it."

14

ALEX

Jenna stares at me from across the table at the coffee shop, an incredulous look on her face, her finger tapping lightly against the cup of tea in front of her.

It's still steaming, filled to the brim. She hasn't taken a sip, hasn't even picked up the cup to go to drink out of it.

"You need to understand," I tell her clearly, really wanting to drive the point home, "that this is over. You and me, we're done. I gave you money for the baby, gave you everything you need to live without having to work, but I don't want to hear from you ever again. This is it."

She stares at me from under her long lashes, blinking slowly like she can't quite believe what I'm saying.

"The money is nice, Alex, but that's not what I want."

"I don't care what you want." I stare at her, half tempted to take her tea from her and drink it myself. I didn't order anything when I got here because she was already in a corner booth, her eyes glued to the door, not even moving when she saw me walk in.

I made a beeline over to her, wanting to get this over

with. She has information that could cause quite a scandal, and I need her to keep it quiet. I have to make her see that telling people isn't an option.

What else can I do to keep her from running her mouth? *Kill her?*

The thought is ridiculous and I shake my head.

"The money is all you get, Jenna. No more emails, no calls, no coming by the house. This is over. I'm happy for you, happy about your baby, and now we are finished."

I stand, already done with this. We met at a quiet coffee shop, and there aren't a lot of people to witness it if she throws a fit, but there are hopefully enough people to keep her from doing anything like that.

"Alex, wait." Jenna stands, reaching across the table and grabbing my wrist.

I freeze.

It's not her hand on my skin that makes me stop dead in my tracks.

It's how big she's gotten.

"When are you due?" I bark the question at her at the same time as she tries to speak.

She frowns. "What?" Without letting go of my wrist, she looks down at her stomach, frowns again, and then looks back up at me.

"Your due date. When is it?"

Letting go of my wrist, she puts her hands on her belly and stares at me. "October third. But why do you care, Alex? A moment ago you couldn't wait to get out of here and never talk to me again."

"You're lying," I tell her. I'm comparing her stomach to Katie's. My wife is still incredibly slim, her stomach almost completely flat. If I didn't know she was pregnant, I wouldn't even guess it.

She keeps chalking it up to so many hours in the Pilates studio and having a great core, but suddenly there's something tugging at the back of my mind.

"Why the hell would I lie about that? Come on, Alex, if I were going to lie about something it sure as hell wouldn't be my due date. Not that I expect to see you at the hospital with flowers or anything." Rolling her eyes, she brushes past me, slamming her shoulder into my arm. "Don't worry, I won't bother you again. I'm happy for you that you get to be a dad. Wish you wanted to be one to our child, too."

A flash of anger washes over me as she walks past me and I turn, watching her leave the coffee shop. She's obviously pregnant and I see a few patrons look up from their drinks and scones, their eyes flicking over her and landing on her belly like they want to enjoy it.

Everyone loves the sight of a pregnant woman. They're a sign of hope for the future.

Why in the world is there such a difference between Jenna and Katie? I look at Jenna and there's no doubt at all that she's pregnant. Why am I not sure of the same thing when I look at Katie?

It's crazy, but suddenly I think that my wife might be lying to me.

Jenna's tea is still on the table and I leave it there, hurrying out to my car. I wasn't here nearly as long as I thought I was going to be, so the baby shower will still be in full swing by the time I get back home. I want to see Katie — really get a good look at her.

I also want to talk to my mother and see what she thinks.

15

KATIE

The smile on Mary's face reminds me of something I've seen on National Geographic.

"Is there something you want to tell me?" Mary leers at me, walking into the bathroom and closing the door behind her. She keeps one hand on the door knob, like she's going to be strong enough to keep someone out if they try to push into the bathroom.

I'm terrified. To be caught by Mary, of all people, makes me feel sick. Part of me really wants to come clean with her and tell her everything, but I don't think I can form the words.

"Nothing to say?" Mary's smile doesn't waver. "Come on, Katie, I think that you'd be crying your heart out if you thought you were losing the baby right now."

Forget the fact that I'm half-naked in front of this woman. That doesn't bother me nearly as much as the way she's looking at me. I know I should be upset about her seeing me like this but my mind is working like a hamster on a wheel, trying to find a way out of this.

I'm not sure there is one.

"Mary, what are you doing in here?" It's the best I can come up with, even though I know it probably isn't a good idea to try to turn this around on her.

She taps her chin with her finger, her nails short so she can keep them clean. There's a flash of something on her face — nerves, maybe — but I don't know why in the world she'd be nervous. She's the one who caught me in the bathroom with my pants down.

Literally.

"There isn't any baby, is there, Katie?" She asks, whispering the words and leaning closer to me.

I strain my ears for any sounds outside. Did anyone else follow me from the baby shower? Was Mary the only one who cared enough to come down the hall after me?

Or has she been waiting for a while now to catch me in a compromising position?

If I was a gambling woman and had to put money on it, that would be my guess. I don't know why she cares so much, but I see Mary watching me more than she should, her eyes following me, her gaze steady and strong. She's been keeping an eye on me and waiting for me to mess up and I just handed myself to her on a silver platter by choosing the bathroom without a lock.

"There was a baby," I tell her. I don't want to admit to her that I failed again, don't want her to know that I've been lying, but I can't lie to her any longer. Lying is exhausting. It makes you paranoid about everyone else around you, makes you think that they're all out to get you.

"And you lost it?" Her voice lilts up at the end of the sentence like she's asking me a question even though I know as well as she does that she's just stating a fact. "You lost the baby and you thought you should just keep lying about it? Why? Do you just love the attention, Katie?"

"No. *No.*" I shake my head so hard my ponytail smacks me in the cheek. "No, I swear to you that's not it. I just couldn't tell Alex. He can't know, Mary, please."

I reach out and grab the woman's hand without realizing there's still blood on mine. She looks down and carefully pulls her hand out of my grasp so as not to get blood on her clothes. As I watch, she goes to the sink and washes up, drying her hands quickly before tossing me the towel.

I catch it and stare at her, unsure of what to do. I know the roles are reversed right now and she has all the power. I also know I have to come clean.

"Let me be the one to tell Alex," I say, and I hate the fact that I sound like begging and I still can't change it. "Please. Let's get through today, get everyone to leave, and then I'll come clean to him. It'll be fine, it'll all be fine." I'm crying, tears dripping off my cheeks and I wipe them away with the towel.

"You're going to tell him you lost the baby and risk him losing the company?" Mary shakes her head, like she can't believe I'd be so stupid. "Where would you be then, Katie? Where, for that matter, would *I* be?"

I stare at her. "You know about all that?"

"I know about everything." She chuckles to herself, then stops. "Well, except this, of course. I mean, I had a feeling you were lying about being pregnant but I hadn't been able to find any proof. You were careful, Katie, that's for sure. But not careful enough."

"So you know that he won't be able to keep the company?"

She nods. "And I know that I'll be out of a job, and you'll be out of this house. What do you think about that?"

The floor feels like it's tilting under my feet as I listen to her words.

"How long have you known?"

She shrugs like we're talking about the weather, not our futures. "About the company? Months. Years. I was just waiting to see if you were going to be able to finally give him the one thing he needed to keep us all in this house."

I wince. "I just found out about it all."

Nodding like she's not surprised, Mary crouches in front of the cupboard and rummages around deeper than I had been able to reach. "Here," she tells me, standing and pressing a tampon and some painkillers into my hands. "Give me your dirty underwear and I'll get rid of it. Use this and get back to your baby shower. You and I have a lot to talk about later."

I feel numb as I nod and take the tampon from her and down two pills without water. She leans back against the door, staring at me.

"You'd better hurry up, Katie. Do you really think Morgana is going to be able to stay away when you've disappeared for so long? This baby is the most important thing ever, and we both know it."

I don't respond as I pull off my pants and remove my underwear. When I ball them up and hand them to her, she takes them and puts them into a rubber glove she had tucked in her pocket and shoves everything deep into a pocket of her apron. I feel self-conscious as I get ready to go back to the party and wash my hands.

"I'll get rid of these," she tells me. "And I'll buy you a little more time, but you and I have some serious talking to do, Katie."

"I know." My lips are cracked, dry, and I lick them, staring at the woman who might be able to help me keep this lie going. “Why in the world do you want to help me, though?”

Her answer is brisk. “I don’t want to be homeless. Besides, I honestly think you losing the baby could be the best thing to ever happen to me.”

16

ALEX

I stride through our kitchen, past the mostly-empty trays of food, ignoring the dozens of cups and glasses that need to be washed, and push the swing door open to the living room.

The chatter subsides as I walk up to Katie, who's sitting next to my mother, a small crystal plate with some finger food balanced on her lap, her eyes locked on the bright primary colored baby bouncer someone just unwrapped for her and put in front of her on the floor.

Ignoring the fact that it's probably the ugliest thing I've ever seen, I step around it and walk up to my wife.

"Katie," I say, and she turns her face up to look at me, a smile on her lips, her cheeks flushed with pleasure. "I need to talk to you."

"Oh, Alex," she says, automatically standing up. "Look at all of the amazing things for the baby. I can't wait to find out if we're having a boy or a girl." She grins at me and hands her plate to my mother. "Will you please hold that, Morgana? Thank you."

I take her hand and lead her out of the room. People

glance at us, but most everyone is too busy eating to see the look on my face.

We step into the kitchen. Mary is at the sink, already running the hot water run to start washing the stuff that can't go in the dishwasher, but I don't care if she hears what I'm going to say to Katie. Mary's been with me for decades and knows the value of keeping her mouth shut. If she's washing dishes she probably won't hear much over the sound of the running water, anyway.

"How are you?" Katie asks, turning to look at me and lightly resting her hand on my chest. "You look a little flustered, Alex, did something happen while you were out?"

I could tell her right now. I could tell her all about Jenna and how different the two of them look. I could come clean with her about everything, about the other baby I have coming, about the problem with the business not passing to me if I don't have a child, but there's no way I can do that.

She'd be pissed, and she'd leave. I married Katie because I fell in love with her and there's no way in the world I'm going to let her go.

"Are you okay?" I answer her question with my own, not ready to talk about what happened at the coffee shop with Jenna. "The baby. Is the baby okay?"

She puts her hand on her perfectly flat stomach and looks up at me, her eyes wide and innocent. "Of course! Why would you ask that? I'm doing everything right, taking my vitamins, skipping out on processed lunch meat, getting enough rest. Why would you wonder if something was wrong?"

She watches me. I watch her. I have a feeling she's not telling me something but how in the world can I get it out of her without her knowing that I'm also lying?

I can't.

"I ran into an old friend when I was out," I say, hedging. . Whatever this charade is, it needs to end. Now. "She's pregnant and due right around your time. I'm only asking because she has quite the stomach on her."

I smile but Katie doesn't.

"Is it her first baby? When women are pregnant a second time then it often shows much sooner than with the first."

"It's her first." I'm sure of it.

"Well, then." Katie exhales and looks concerned. "Do you think there's something wrong with our baby? Do you think we need to be worried?"

I stare at her. How in the world could I think my wife would lie to me about something like this? She's so kind, so pure. That's what really attracted me to her after I met her at the café. Sure, at first it was all physical, but then I learned more about Katie and how good her heart is. That's why I decided I had to have her, had to have her as the mother of my child.

"I don't think anything's *wrong*," I tell her, seeing that she's about to freak out. "I just got worried when I ran into Jenna."

There's a flash of something on Katie's face when I say Jenna's name, but it's gone before I can recognize what it is. But I'd swear I saw something there.

Just for a moment.

"I'm so sorry to interrupt," Mary says, walking over as she dries her hands on a towel, "but I'll admit I was a little worried about Katie too. At first. I'm not anymore, though." She smiles and lightly touches my wife on the arm.

Katie doesn't move.

"What do you mean?" I'm irritated that Mary feels comfortable inserting herself in our conversation, but at the same time I really want to hear what she has to say. Maybe she knows something I don't.

"There are so many stories online about women who didn't know they were pregnant," Mary says, and squeezes Katie's arm before stepping back to look at her. "Your wife is incredible. Have you looked at her? She's obviously carrying this pregnancy really well if we can barely tell. Though to be honest I noticed you've gained a bit of a tummy, Katie."

Katie looks surprised but only for a moment before she nods. "You saw that too? I think I need to size up in my jeans finally. It's probably because I keep throwing up that I'm not gaining any weight, but you can definitely see a bit of a pooch when I turn to the side. Look."

As if to prove her point, Katie turns, pulling her clothing tight against her stomach.

"See?" She rubs her hand across the small little bump there, sounding breathless as she does.

Breathless. She's excited.

"Yes, I see it," I say, rubbing her stomach. Katie waits until I pull my hand back, then she exhales hard, letting her shirt fall back down. "I hadn't noticed it before."

"You've been so busy," she tells me, leaning up to give me a kiss. "I don't expect you to notice every little detail of my pregnancy. All that matters to me is that you love this baby."

"Oh, I will." Gathering her in my arms, I hug her. "I'm sorry I was worried. I just saw someone else and I thought that maybe there was something wrong."

I thought you were lying to me.

"Nothing's wrong," she says, snuggling into my chest. "There are a million reasons why one person might be showing more or less than another."

"I want you to get another ultrasound," I tell her, pulling back a bit and looking at her. "I think that's the best way to put my mind at ease and make sure we're all comfortable with how you and the baby are doing."

She chews her lower lip. "Do you really think that's necessary? Our insurance isn't going to cover a random ultrasound."

"I don't care about the money. What I care about is making sure the baby is fine. And you too, of course."

She nods, pulling the rest of the way away from me. "Okay, I'll call tomorrow." She glances at Mary and gives her a small nod, then turns and walks back through the doors into the living room to rejoin her party.

I don't say anything as she goes, but it's the weirdest thing ...

I would have thought Katie would be thrilled to see our baby again.

So why isn't she?

17

KATIE

I wait until Alex leaves the house the next morning before going to find Mary. It's inevitable, the conversation the two of us have to have, but that doesn't mean I really want to sit down with her and try to figure out what exactly she knows.

And, more importantly, what she wants.

It feels like she knows everything, and I hate that. I hate feeling like someone else knew more than I did about something involving me in my own house.

But if she can come up with a way out of this problem, then I'll gladly listen to her.

I just hope I can trust her?

She's cleaning up the living room where we had the baby shower yesterday, making sure all of the little bits of confetti and shreds of tissue paper are up off the floor and thrown away. Alex hates messy rooms and I'm sure it took all of his self-control not to complain about the state of the room when everyone finally left.

It was supposed to be just an afternoon event, but then

everyone kept dipping into the champagne and it stretched out well into the evening.

Whatever. It's done now. All of the baby gifts are stacked against one wall in the living room. There are piles of clothes that I should dig through and lay out, smoothing out the wrinkles on my lap as I look at them. I should put batteries in everything and shake the little rattles. I should compare the sizes of the diapers.

It's what I'd do if I was really pregnant.

"Sit with me," I say to Mary, handing her a cup of tea I just brewed. "We need to talk."

There's a smile on her face I don't really like but she takes the tea and we settle into two wing-back chairs by the fireplace. I curl up in the chair, doing my best to look calm. The painkillers I've been taking since the baby shower are doing their job, reducing my painful cramps to more of a dull ache instead of the feeling that something is shredding me from the inside.

"We do indeed." She blows on her tea and takes a sip. "You're not pregnant?"

I sigh and shake my head. She knows this, and why she wants to go through it like this, I'm not sure, but I have a very good feeling it has something to do with control and how badly she wants it.

"And Alex doesn't know?"

"He can't know."

She nods. "No, he can't. He'd lose it, Katie, if he thought you had miscarried again. He needs an heir to keep the company."

The conversation is getting off track already but I can't help the question that springs to my lips. "How do you know all of that, anyway?"

She shrugs, like it's no big deal. "I've been with the family a long time, Katie. Much longer than you. I hear things. There isn't enough space in a house to hold all of the secrets of the people who live there. They all surface eventually."

I drink some tea. It's the perfect temperature and I know I should be enjoying it, but I barely taste it as I watch Mary. When she doesn't immediately speak, I know I have to come up with something to keep the conversation going.

"Are you going to tell Alex?"

"No." Her answer is immediate and definite, and honestly it surprises me a little.

"Are you going to make me tell Alex?"

"No." Now there's a hint of amusement in her voice. "Do you really think I want to do that, Katie? I told you yesterday: I like living here and working here. I want to stay, and you and your husband want to stay too. The only way for us to all get what we want is for there to be a baby."

"But I don't *have* a baby," I say, feeling desperate. We could go around in circles like this all day long and never get anywhere. "That's the problem, that's—"

She cuts me off. "But I do."

"What?" I'm gripping the mug so hard that my fingers feel like they're starting to cramp and I have to focus on relaxing my grip a little bit. "What do you mean *you have a baby*?"

"Just what I said. I know of a baby who needs a home. A baby that you could love as your own. It's a simple adoption. There won't even be any paperwork."

"That's illegal. It has to be."

She shrugs. "So? The mother needs someone to take care of the baby and you need a baby. Why send this poor child to an orphanage when you could just open your arms and your home and take it in? Simple."

This is insane. Putting my tea down on the table between us, I start to stand up, then I sit back down. My legs feel weak, like they could easily give out under me at any time. Bringing my legs up to my chest, I wrap my arms around them and pull them tight to me.

"You couldn't do that so easily if you were pregnant," she points out.

"Mary, please. You already know I'm not." I snap, trying to think through what she told me.

I need a baby, or I need to come clean with Alex, and I don't think I can do that.

Someone out there has a baby they want to find a home for, a home where they know the baby will be loved.

Why shouldn't I be the person to love that baby? Why shouldn't it come to live with me, live in this incredible home, live with parents who will do whatever it takes to make sure the baby has the best possible life?

"I have something that might help you decide." Mary pulls a small envelope from a pocket on the front of her apron and hands it to me. For a moment, I don't want to take it, but then I stretch my hand out and take the envelope in my fingers.

"What is it?"

She doesn't answer and I finally pull out a small piece of paper from inside the envelope. It has a familiar feel to it. It's not computer paper, exactly, it's . . .

"The ultrasound your husband wants you to have to make sure you're really pregnant. Of course, I cut the girl's name off the side and removed the date, but this should work, don't you think?"

I can't speak. Tracing my finger across the black print on the paper, I wish more than anything that this was really mine. I would have loved to have gone to the doctor, felt the cold jelly on my stomach, seen the little heartbeat for myself.

Someone else got to do that, not me.

Why in the world shouldn't I help them out?

"Who's the mom?" I ask, not taking my eyes away from the ultrasound. I can't look away. It's like the black ink and swirls on the page have suddenly become my entire life.

"That's confidential. She doesn't want anyone to know who she is."

I look up at Mary, forcing myself to tear my eyes away from the ultrasound. "What does she want? Money? I don't want to buy a baby, don't want to do anything illegal."

"She has money. Doesn't want more. And it's not illegal, Katie, it's just you opening your heart to a child who needs a family. Don't you see? This baby is your future and all you have to do is let them in. You just have to say yes and I'll make sure you have all of the proof you need of being pregnant to keep Alex happy. Then, in a few months, you'll have your very own baby to hold and love. Everybody wins."

"You're sure the mother won't change her mind?" The thought is unimaginable. How many horror stories have I read about adoptions going wrong and that exact thing happening? "I couldn't do that. Couldn't give the baby back."

"It won't be a problem." Mary sounds so calm, so sure of herself, that I actually start to believe that maybe this can work. "Once the baby is yours, the baby is yours. Your due dates are close together, and the baby will be born when Alex is away. When he gets home, you'll have a child."

"He'll never believe it." My voice is soft as I try to convince myself this is a terrible idea.

But oh, how badly I want it to work.

Do I dare?

"He'll believe it because he wants to." Mary sounds

confident and raises her eyebrow when I look up at her. "Think about it. Do you really think he'll argue with you when he comes home and you have the baby he's been wanting so badly?"

"You're right. He won't." I start to sound confident, too. Mary is making me feel better about this. "He won't ask questions, he'll just be happy."

"Exactly. You'll have the baby you both want so badly and we won't have to worry about what will happen with the company."

"And the baby's mom? You're *sure* she's on board with this?"

Mary smiles and the sight gives me chills. I've always believed in listening to your gut and there's a voice in the back of my head screaming at me right now that I'm making a huge mistake, but I push it away.

I should listen to that voice, but I don't want to.

"Trust me, Katie, nothing terrible is going to happen. This is the best option we have for everyone getting what they want. What do you say? Are you going to give Alex the ultrasound?"

The ultrasound. I'll have to come up with some reason why I cut the name and date off, but I'll think of something. Maybe he won't even notice.

Then, knowing full well this might be a terrible idea, I nod.

"I'll give him the ultrasound."

18

ALEX

"I took your advice, and I'm so glad I did," Katie says, sitting down next to me at the dining room table.

We've always sat across from each other when we eat, so for her to sit next to me is a little strange. Her food is across the table all ready for her and everything. Still, I'm interested in what advice of mine she could have taken and I reach out without thinking to take the piece of paper she's handing me.

"You got another ultrasound?" I don't want to sound surprised, but there's part of me that honestly can't believe she did that. Seeing Jenna got into my head and made me think that maybe there was something wrong with my wife and the baby, but if this piece of paper is any indication, there isn't.

She's just smaller, just taking longer to show.

Just like Mary told me.

"I did." Katie nods and leans her head on my shoulder, reaching out to trace her finger lightly over the little black smudge in the middle of the paper. "I did, and I'm so glad.

You were right. Getting to see the baby, getting to know that they're okay, that's all I wanted."

"Amazing." I kiss her, dropping the paper down on the table. It doesn't look exactly like the one she had on the refrigerator before, but I can't put my finger on what it is. "Did they say if we're having a boy or a girl?"

She shakes her head. "No. I wasn't sure if we wanted to know or if we wanted to find out as a surprise. A lot of people are doing that now, waiting until the baby is actually born to name them and tell everyone what it was." She pauses and tilts her head to look at me. "What do you think?"

"I'd like to know, but I can wait if that's what you want." I'm not sure what it is, but I'm feeling kinder towards Katie than I have in a while. There's something about the fact that she went and got the ultrasound without complaining that makes me love her even more.

I have to keep reminding myself that this must be scary for her. She's been pregnant a handful of times and never been able to keep the baby. The fact that this one is sticking has to be both exciting and terrifying as she looks every single day for any hint that she might lose this one, too.

Maybe I haven't been as tuned in to her as I should have been. Maybe she's been feeling all alone and scared and I just haven't noticed because I've been wrapped up in my own life, worried about if we were going to have an heir, worried about everything with Jenna.

But that's all over.

Since meeting at the coffee shop, I haven't heard from her. I don't know what it was that I finally said to her to make her back off, but she doesn't want anything to do with me now. I even emailed her this morning offering her more money, just in case she was thinking about doing something stupid and possibly turning me in to Katie and letting her know the truth, but nothing. No response.

Radio silence.

It made me nervous at first, but now it just makes me happy. I have her out of my life, finally, and Katie and I are going to have a baby.

At last.

"If you do decide that you want to know if it's a boy or a girl ahead of time then I'd like to be there at the ultrasound," I say, and even though it's there and gone in a flash, I see the surprise on Katie's face.

"I know I haven't always been around because I've been working so hard," I tell her, taking her by the chin and turning her face so she's looking at me, "but this is important to me. I'm not going to let you go through all of this on your own. I want to be there. I want to be an involved father, okay?"

"You're incredible," she says, smiling and then standing to walk around the table to her seat. She settles in her chair before speaking again. "Hmm. I think I want it to be a surprise."

"Whatever you want, sweetheart." Strange, I got the feeling a moment ago that she *didn't* want to wait to find out what the baby was, but maybe I'm just so worried about this baby not surviving that I'm putting my thoughts on her. "It's all about you, Katie."

She smiles at me and puts her hand on her stomach.

Does it look bigger?

"It's really all about the baby. Don't worry, Alex, you know I wouldn't do anything that isn't for the best of our baby. I've wanted this child for so long, and to know that we're going to be parents after all this time . . . it's the best feeling ever."

"It is." I can't take my eyes from her. She's simply glowing. That's something I always thought was a myth people told pregnant women to make them feel better about the fact that they were getting big as a house and having trouble moving, but it's true.

Katie is glowing. Sure, she's thin. Sure, I honestly can't see a belly yet and I don't think she's wearing maternity clothes, but what does that matter? The only thing that's important to me is making sure we have a healthy baby we can love and who can grow up and inherit the family business.

Hell, at this point I don't even care if the child doesn't want to go into investments like I did. The fact that we'll have an heir is all that really matters. That way the company will stay mine.

Katie wants this baby, though. She's wanted to be a mother since I met her, and every time we lose one it's been harder and harder on her. For a while, I thought that I was going to lose her to the crushing sadness that kept falling over her like a thick snow each month, but she's managed to find her way out of that sadness now, and it's because of the baby she's carrying.

So she needs this baby to survive, to love, to hold and to cherish.

I know she's being careful. I know she's doing all the right things.

But if she loses this baby, I honestly don't know what I'll do.

19

KATIE

JULY

The time when I'd have an ultrasound to determine the gender of our child comes and goes and I continue to make pretend appointments, writing them on the calendar and circling them in green, drawing little hearts, and making sure I'm out of the house at those times.

It's not that I really think Alex would come by the house looking for me to make sure that I'm not really here when I'm supposed to be at an appointment, but what if he had an inkling that something was wrong and came to check and I was here? No bueno.

Not long to go now. I've gotten this down to a fine art. I've learned how to press my stomach out when I'm around Alex, how to inhale and hold the air so that my stomach gets tight and looks larger. At night I pore over baby books and complain about the ailments that are supposedly affecting me.

I talk about feeling the baby move. Getting heartburn. Being unable to sleep well at night.

I know what's coming in the future, like my feet growing

in size and not fitting into my current shoes, like finding stretch marks and applying cream to them to keep them from growing, like noticing that my hair gets thicker softer.

Rolling my shoulders back, I step away from the wall and admire the paint job I've done. The nursery is a soft yellow. *Buttercup*, it says on the can. It's cheery and light and the white curtains make the room look like it's from a fairytale.

Alex told me we could hire someone to paint the room, but I said I wanted to do it myself. Even though it isn't going to be mine, I'm going to have a baby in the house soon, and I'm feeling antsy, like I need to be involved in every part of getting ready for its arrival.

The sound of the door opening makes me turn around and I tense, but Mary walks through the door, a smile on her face, her head cocked to the side.

"Looking good," she tells me, crossing her arms and admiring my handiwork. "We can get the crib and rocker moved in here tomorrow and you'll finally have a place for everything you got at the baby shower."

"Sounds good." Stretching my back, I put the paintbrush down on the lid of the can.

"How's the baby?" I ask, dropping my voice as low as I can and stepping closer to Mary. I don't think Alex is home yet or he'd already be up here to see how the painting is going, but I don't want to risk him overhearing us.

It's just not worth it.

"She's good," Mary tells me with a smile, and I reach up, covering my mouth before I realize what I'm doing.

"She?"

Mary nods. "She. You're having a little girl, Katie. How does that feel?"

It feels amazing. It feels like everything I've ever

wanted is finally coming true and even though I know I can't ruin it by being happy, part of me is afraid to get too excited in case everything comes crashing down around me.

In case the baby's mother backs out.

"You don't think she's going to change her mind? The mom?" I can't help the touch of fear I hear in my voice and even though I hope Mary won't hear it, it's obvious from the smile on her face that she does.

She puts her arm around my shoulder, which surprises me, even though I've known her for a long time now and it's nice to have someone want to take care of me. I don't have a lot of friends.

"Believe me," she says, leaning her head over so it's touching mine. "The mom wants what's best for her daughter, and she knows that coming to this family is the best chance for the little girl to get the life she deserves."

Her words send a chill down my spine. "I'm sorry, but does the mom know who I am? Did you tell her where the baby would be going?" For some reason, I really don't like that.

My biggest fear all along has been that the mom would come back in the future and try to take the baby away from Alex and me. If she knows who we are and where the baby is, that's totally possible.

"Oh, no, I'm sorry, she doesn't know who you are, just that the baby will have a much better life with you. That's what I meant. Don't worry, Katie, I'm taking care of everything. All you have to do is open your arms and your home and love this little girl and everything will be fine."

We're silent for a moment, the two of us both lost in our own thoughts. I'm not sure what Mary is thinking but all I can imagine is how amazing it's going to be to hold my baby.

Even though she's not going to be from my body, does it matter?

I don't think so. And Alex will never know. That's the most important thing.

"And we really don't need paperwork, right?" It's a concern I've had but haven't felt comfortable voicing yet. "If there's any paperwork then other people might find out."

"No paper trail. This mom isn't in a place where she can argue. She needs help. You're giving her a gift, and you'll be loving her daughter. Don't worry."

I'm about to triple-check with her, about to ask her if she's totally sure, but suddenly we're no longer alone in the nursery.

"Well, isn't this is cozy." Alex's voice startles me and I jump, pulling away from Mary and trying not to look like I have something to hide.

"Hey, you," I say, walking over to him. I take a deep breath, pressing my stomach out as far as I can. It's not very far, even though I've been doing my best to eat more during the day, especially stuff that makes me bloat. The scale is inching higher, but very slowly. If I were really pregnant then I'd be packing on the pounds by now.

Ten pounds isn't going to kill me and it will only make this seem more real to everyone else.

"Did you do all of this today?" Alex kisses me, his lips soft against mine, and I nod as I turn under his arm to look around the room.

"Yep. And before you ask, it's low VOC paint so you don't have to worry. I just finished and Mary came in to check it out." Turning, I grin up at him. "This baby is going to be so loved. I can't wait to meet her."

As soon as the words are out of my mouth, I realize what I just said.

I stiffen, wishing I could melt into the floor or take it back.

The very air in the room seems tight and heavy, like I'm underwater and I can't get enough oxygen into my lungs to keep from feeling like I'm drowning.

Alex turns to me, his brow furrowed.

"Her?"

20

ALEX

Katie doesn't respond.

"Katie. You said *her.* Do you know that we're having a girl?"

A little girl is not what I really wanted, but does it matter in the long run? What matters to me is having an heir, living flesh and blood, some child I can parade around so I can keep the business and more to the point the income that it provides me.

Katie looks like she's about to choke. Her eyes are wide and she looks at Mary before turning to look back at me. Her mouth drops open slightly and I stare at her, willing her to speak, but it's like any words she was going to use have disappeared, rendering her absolutely speechless.

"We were just talking about it," Mary says, walking over and putting her arm around Katie's shoulders again. They were standing like that when I walked into the room, like the two of them were incredible friends and wanted nothing more than to be close to each other.

When did Mary and Katie get this close?

"And you think it's a girl?" I can't help the surprise in my voice. I know I need to be more supportive, or calm, or some damned thing, but there's worry eating away at the back of my mind that I can't shake and I'm not sure where it's coming from. "Why would you think that?"

"Oh, it's silly," Mary says, and I notice that she's speaking for my wife but I don't know what to say to her to give Katie a chance to answer me herself. "You're going to think it's just an old wives' tale."

"Try me."

Katie swallows and glances at Mary. "In some of the books I've been reading, they talk about how you can guess if you're having a boy or a girl without an ultrasound. It's not a sure thing, not like an ultrasound, more a fun little game the two of us were playing."

I'm not convinced. "How does it work?"

"You take a wedding ring," Katie says, twisting hers off her finger to show me, "and loop a string through it so it can hang. Then I got on the floor and Mary held the ring above my stomach. It sways back and forth and side to side and will kinda choose a direction."

"And that tells you if you're having a girl or a boy?" I can't keep the derision out of my voice.

Katie shrugs. "I mean, it's not like I necessarily believe it, but it's kinda fun and it was just a cute little thing to do."

An uncomfortable silence falls, then Mary speaks up. "Wouldn't it be funny if you did have a girl, though? Like, it would be really neat. I'm not counting it out. You never know what's going to happen."

"You really don't." Katie smiles at her, and as she turns away from me, I have the perfect opportunity to really look at my wife. I hadn't noticed before, but she's finally putting on a little weight.

It's not a bad thing. She looks healthier than she has in a

while. I like it. Her cheeks, which are usually pretty hollow, seem to have filled out. She's carrying a bit more weight in her stomach, which I'm happy to see. Finally we'll get the baby bump that she's been waiting for.

"You look beautiful," I tell her, taking her hand in mine and giving her fingers a squeeze. "Healthy. And I don't care if it's a boy or a girl as long as they're healthy, too."

"Same." She smiles up at me and then turns to look at Mary. "Thanks again for doing that with me. It was a little silly, but fun."

"It was." Carefully, like she doesn't want to bump into Katie, Mary walks around the two of us. "I'll see you two tomorrow. You are going to make great parents, I can feel it."

"Bye, Mary!" Katie waves at her and then turns back to me. "What do you think about the nursery, Alex?"

"It looks great." I'm honestly not sure about the color and wouldn't have chosen it if it had been up to me, but if this is what my wife really wanted for the nursery, then I'm fine with it. All that matters is that there's a baby in the crib when I get back from Europe.

"You really like it?"

I nod and she grins.

"Good, I'm glad. All that painting worked up an appetite. Or maybe baby here really just likes chicken and dumplings. Oh, and brownies. I did a lot of baking today before I started painting because I knew I was going to be really hungry." Katie tugs my hand as she heads towards the door. "You ready for some dinner?"

"Sounds good." I let my wife lead me down the hall, but although I'm walking with her and half-listening to what she's saying, I'm off in my own world, thinking about the nursery, remembering the silly little game she and Mary played to find out if we are going to have a boy or a girl.

It's one thing to just guess, but Katie sounded like she really *knew*. I was surprised, not only because of how confident she seemed in it, but because I thought we were on the same page about not finding out until the birth.

Sure, I don't love the idea of not knowing now, but maybe that's not the end of the world.

Then again, if she's playing around with old wives' tales to find out if we're having a boy or a girl, she might be open to getting an ultrasound so we can know for sure. I bet I can ask her and get her to agree to one.

At least that way I'll know before I leave the country. I won't have to worry about expecting one thing and getting the other. I hate it when that happens.

I sit at the counter while she dishes up two steaming bowls of chicken and dumplings and slices two thick pieces of bread to go with it.

"You're really feeling the carbs today, huh?" I ask, taking my bowl from her.

"The baby is." Katie laughs, sounding and looking happier than she has in a while. "I'm just giving her what she wants." She sits down next to me and it hits me that we rarely eat in the kitchen like this. I look around, trying to imagine what it will be like to have a highchair here next to us in just a few months, the one from the baby shower, soft tan with green stripes. "I want you to get an ultrasound," I tell Katie, turning to look at her right as she puts a bite in her mouth. "I want to know if we're having a boy or a girl. I'll come with you."

She chokes on a dumpling.

21

KATIE

My back is still sore from where Alex pounded on it last night to dislodge the dumpling that got stuck in my throat.

The last thing I expected to hear him say was that he wanted to get an ultrasound before he left, and the shock still hasn't left me. I know I need to get over it and figure out what I'm going to do to keep him at bay, but I'm not quite sure what to do. .

Right now, I'm waiting for Mary to get here. She might not have all the answers, but she should have the ones I need, and I have to trust that she can help me.

Alex left for work an hour ago and my second cup of coffee isn't doing the job so I walk into the kitchen, pour a healthy slug of Bailey's into the mug, then take another pull from the bottle for good measure.

"God, that's good," I say, carefully screwing the cap back on and replacing the bottle in the cupboard above the refrigerator. The last thing I need is to accidentally leave it out and have Alex pop home to check on me.

Hurrying back to the front door, I decide to wait on the

front porch for Mary, and I step outside right as she pulls up in her little white Corolla. My nerves are on edge as I wait for her to walk up to the porch, then I grab hold of her arm.

"I need a picture of an ultrasound that clearly shows it's a girl," I tell her. I'm squeezing her hard, probably too hard, but this is important. Alex is going to call later and ask when my appointment will be and I need to have something I can tell him.

Mary looks down at where I'm squeezing her arm, then gently but firmly pries my fingers away. "What's the rush? Yesterday you weren't going to tell Alex and then you let it slip." Mary presses her lips together in a thin line, looking disappointed in me.

"Yes, it slipped. I didn't mean for it to, but it did, and now Alex wants to know for sure and he wants to go with me to the doctor's office to see the ultrasound. So I need a picture. Now."

"Okay, okay, slow down, let me think." She takes a step back from me, eyeballing me like she thinks I've suddenly gone crazy. Maybe she's right.

I take another sip of my coffee and close my eyes as I swallow gratefully. I'm really not a huge drinker, but desperate times call for desperate measures and all that.

"I can get you an ultrasound picture," Mary tells me, leading me into the house. "But you have to — Jesus, are you *drinking*? Give me that." She takes my mug from me and sniffs it, frowning. "That is really not okay, Katie. What if Alex were to stop by to check on you?"

I shrug. "I needed something to calm down."

"Then try yoga," she snaps. I raise my eyebrows, then she shakes her head apologetically. "I'm sorry, this is just more stressful than I thought it would be."

A mirthless laugh bursts from my lips. "You didn't think

lying to my husband and taking an unwanted baby from someone else without legal documentation wouldn't be stressful?"

Mary nods her head, thinking aloud. "Okay, this is what we have to do. I'll get you the picture, okay? I'll see if the mom can drop it off for me here, and then you'll text Alex in a bit and tell him that you had to go in this morning or you wouldn't have been able to get an appointment anytime soon. You got a cancellation, yes, that's it. Then you'll tell him it's a girl."

"You don't think he'll call the doctor to check up on me?" I feel hot and sweaty. The thermostat is in the hall and I walk back a few feet to lower the temperature a few degrees. "To double-check, I mean. Do you think he'd do that?"

"Do *you*?" Mary stares at me. She's put my coffee cup and her purse on the counter and has her phone out in her hands like she's ready to make a call. "He's your husband, Katie, you tell me." Then her tone softens. "Look, I'm willing to help you do this, but right now you seem like you want to back out."

"No, I don't. There's no way out of this except with that baby. You get the ultrasound here and then I'll let Alex know that it's already been done. He'll probably be grateful that he doesn't have to leave the office after all."

"He's leaving soon for his trip, right?" Mary's fingers fly on her phone and I'm tempted to try to see who she's texting. I'm dying to know who the mom is and even though meeting her isn't a good idea,

Still, I'm curious.

"Soonish. Less than two months. This pregnancy really has flown by." The words are out of my mouth before I realize what I'm saying.

Mary stares at me as she puts her phone back in her

pocket. Then she smiles. "You play the part really well, you know that?"

I feel my face start to burn but I manage to hold her gaze. "What, the part of being a pregnant woman? It's because I've decided I am." I know I'm being ridiculous but I can't help it. I already realized that the more I believed that I was actually pregnant, the more likely other people would fall for it, too.

"Well, you're convincing. Even how you stand. You're doing better about making it look like you have a bit of a belly. But your boobs need work. Have you thought about stuffing your bra?"

"Should I?" The thought hadn't even crossed my mind, but it's not like Alex would find out. He's been . . . hands-off . . . since we found out I was pregnant, because he was afraid of hurting the baby. Still, that seems like a little too much information to share with Mary, so I keep it to myself.

"Yes, I think you should. Stuff the bra, try to put on a little more weight. You still fit in your old clothes. Get some maternity clothes that tie under your boobs. That will make you look pregnant. It's time to shake up the wardrobe, Katie."

"Alex leaves pretty soon though," I point out.

"Yeah, and don't you want him to be totally convinced that you're pregnant when he goes? Trust me, Katie. I'll get you the ultrasounds you need and the baby, but you have to really sell it." She sounds so sure of herself that I feel my back straighten a little bit.

"You're right," I tell her, and I nod, more to convince myself than her of what I'm saying. "I thought I was doing enough, but I guess I need to do more."

I think about how carefully I've hidden it when I get my period. Mary has been helpful there, making sure to take out the bathroom trash regularly, ensuring that he won't ever be able to find any evidence that I'm not pregnant. I've been putting on more weight, continuing to complain about the right ailments that a pregnant woman would be dealing with, and making sure to talk about how excited I am about the baby.

He sees all of it, I know he does, but Mary is right, I need to do more.

There's a part of me that still really wants to know who our baby's mother is, but I keep pushing that thought away. I trust Mary. She could have turned me over to Alex a hundred times by now and made this all come crashing down at my feet, but she hasn't, and honestly, I believe she's going to be with me to the end.

Today will be a big test of how the final act of this will go.

22

ALEX

MID-SEPTEMBER

The next time the ultrasound appeared on the refrigerator, I was happy to leave it up there. Normally it drives me nuts to have clutter in the house, but I knew it was important to Katie.

A girl.

We're having a little girl.

The game that she and Mary played to try to find out what we were having seemed to have been right, and she was over the moon about that. I've never seen Katie this happy.

It has to be because the baby is so close to being born. We're closer to actually becoming parents than we ever have been before. In the past we've been close but we've lost it towards the end, had that life ripped away from us.

How many times have we gotten pregnant only to lose the baby? There's only so many times a person can go through grief like that. I'm honestly impressed that Katie has been holding it together as well as she has.

Other women might have done something drastic by now. Not that I think Katie would go so far as to try to kidnap someone's baby from their cart at the grocery store or anything. At least she finally stopped mentioning adoption, and for that, I'm grateful.

I'm robotically packing clothes when a knock on the bedroom door makes me look up. Katie's standing there, one hand on her stomach, a maternity top tied tightly under her breasts. She's put on weight up top and in the cheeks, her face filling out a little bit more. She looks terrific.

"You're a sight for sore eyes," I say, dropping the socks I was holding into my suitcase and gesturing for her to join me. "Come over here, Katie."

"I just wanted to see how it was going," she says, then walks to the bed and perches on the edge of it, groaning a little as she sits and rubbing her back. "It's hard to stay for too long in any one position. It's like my entire body stiffens up and I need to move around to work it all out again."

"I want you to see about a pregnancy massage," I tell her, grabbing more socks from the dresser and stuffing them into my suitcase. They're the last things I have to pack. "You're in your third trimester, there's no reason to wait until Anna is born. If you don't feel good, get a massage. We can easily afford one."

"Thanks." She flashes me a smile and turns to the side, lightly stretching before she speaks again. "I'm really going to miss you, you know. I hate that you're not going to be here when Anna is born."

"I hate it, too." Just like I hated it when she went to the doctor without me for her last ultrasound. I meant it when I told her I wanted to be there for that, that I wanted to be a part of finding out if we were having a boy or a girl. The fact that she would go without me, even though it was apparently a last-minute appointment, still stings.

I would have taken time off work to join her.

I would have tried, at least.

"Don't forget my mother has offered to be there with you if you want her," I say, watching Katie's expression as I speak. It shifts, just a little. A small frown.

"I'm not sure that I want her there," Katie tells me slowly. She sounds apologetic and I turn from her, pressing my clothes down in my suitcase to make sure they all fit. She can see that I'm a little upset by what she just said and she reaches out, lightly touching my arm.

"I'm sorry, Alex. I just want this to be as calm as possible. If you can't be there with me then I don't know that I want anyone else there. Of course I'll call her as soon as Anna's born, and I've talked to you."

"She's going to be heartbroken," I say. "I'm not going to make you do something you're not comfortable with, but I want you to know that. She really loves you."

She loves the idea of an heir.

"I know. And as soon as Anna and I are home and are settled in, Morgana is going to be the first person I call to come visit. I promise, okay?"

She sounds so earnest that I stop and walk to her, taking her hands in mine and squeezing them. Even though she's told me time and time again that she doesn't feel very sexy right now, I kiss her, lightly cupping her cheek so she can't pull away. I want my wife, I want to say goodbye to her the way a man should before leaving for a few months.

"It's going to be so hard not to be here," I tell her, kissing her harder. She kisses back, but then pulls away.

I want more.

"I love you, Katie," I tell her, pushing her back to try to make her lie down on the bed. "Let me show you how much I love you."

"Alex, I love you too, but no." Katie plants her hands behind her on the bed, forcing herself to sit up, making it impossible for me to push her all the way back. "I promise you, things will go back to normal between us after Anna gets here." She puts her hand on my chest and digs her fingers into my skin through my clothes. "I miss you in that way, I really do, but now is not the time."

I pull away from her in frustration, running my hand through my hair. Then my eyes fall on the clock across the room.

Damn, I need to get moving.

"I'll see you when I get back," I say, zipping up my suitcase. The sound is loud in the quiet of the room and Katie slips from the bed, suddenly grabbing her side.

"Oh," she says, and I'm suddenly filled with memories of all the other times I've heard her make that noise when she moves suddenly during pregnancy. All I can see when I look at her right now are the number of times she's crumpled to the floor, sobbing as she cramps, sobbing as she loses the baby.

"Katie." Grabbing her, I lift her up, pulling her to my chest. "Katie, what is it? Is it the baby?"

"I think it's just gas," she says, exhaling hard as she bends over to the side, her hand gripping her side so hard her fingers sink into her flesh. "Don't worry about me, okay?"

She gives me a reassuring smile and I know I shouldn't worry. My wife will be fine. The baby will be fine. We have the best medical team on board to take care of them no matter what happens, Mary too. Katie's far enough along that even if the baby came early, it would be fine in a preemie ward. I'm sure I read that somewhere.

And yet...and yet...

I've never thought that Katie was lying to me, but right now I can't shake the feeling that she's not telling me the truth.

23

KATIE

I manage to keep it together until Alex is out the door, his rolling suitcase in one hand, his carry-on on the other. I watch the sleek black town car he hired to pick him up and take him to the airport pull away from the house and then slam the door, throw the lock, and rush to the bathroom.

Mary stands behind me, one eyebrow raised, a knowing look on her face as I hurry past her down the hall.

That was close. What if it had been five minutes earlier, and Alex had seen that I was bleeding? There wasn't any way he'd have gotten on that plane, no matter what I said to him or how hard I tried to push him.

And then everything I've been working for would have fallen apart in just two seconds as my lie came crashing down.

I finish up in the bathroom and wash my hands, walking to the kitchen to join Mary. She's leaning on the counter, her arms crossed, a grin on her face. "You barely made it."

I feel like she's laughing at me and I study her face. It's

calm now, composed. "It's a good thing I did. You would have gone down with me had he found out the truth."

"You know we both want this too badly to let that happen." She turns away from me, filling the electric kettle and fitting it on its base before flipping the switch and turning back to me. "What are you going to do now?"

Good question. I'm not sure. I love it when Alex travels because it means I get to stay up later than normal watching crap TV, eating ice cream out of the carton, and sleeping in. This time it's different.

"I guess it depends on Anna," I say. "When is she coming? When is she due?"

While Mary grabs two mugs and drops tea bags in them, I wipe my hands on my pants. I'm nervous, although I don't know why. This was always the plan.

"Just over two weeks." Mary finally turns and hands me my mug. It's too hot to handle and I have to shift how I'm holding it and grab it by the handle so I don't burn my hands. "You have a little more than two weeks and then you'll have a baby. When she's born I'll go to the hospital and help the mother, then she'll go home and I'll bring the baby here."

"Maybe I could go with you to the hospital," I begin, but Mary shakes her head.

"No. She doesn't want to meet you," she says firmly, and even though I'm a little disappointed, I understand.

"Two weeks," I repeat, trying the words out to see how they feel. "That means Anna will be older when Alex gets back. I thought the due date was closer to when he got home." Suddenly I see a huge wrench that could be thrown right into our plans. It's one thing to think that Alex wouldn't notice that a newborn wasn't his.

An older baby is something else.

"It'll be fine," Mary tells me, taking a sip of her tea. It's too hot for me to even imagine letting it touch my tongue and I wince a little as I watch her drink her steaming brew. "I have no doubt in my mind that Alex will believe that this is your child. After all, you've kept him believing the lie this far, right?"

She reaches out and rubs my arm. "I'll be here for you every step of the way, Katie. I'm not going to abandon you and make you deal with this on your own, okay?"

"Okay." I swallow hard. "It's just a lot. And what if I don't bond with Anna? What if I struggle?"

"We'll hire a nanny." Mary sounds very confident. I turn to her, looking to see if she's serious.

She is.

"A nanny?" I'm a little unsure of this, even though it is something I've thought about. Even Alex mentioned it once, but I had hoped to be the kind of supermom who could handle anything and everything thrown at her without any help.

But look at me. I can't even get a baby without help.

"A nanny, sure. I think it's a great idea."

"Gosh, but I wouldn't even know how to find one. That sounds like the most daunting prospect in the world." Sighing, I blow on my tea a bit more. It's still really hot but I take a small sip.

"Yes, but I do. That's the secret about housekeepers."

I cock an eyebrow at her. "What? That you guys run an underground nanny network?"

This makes her laugh. "Hardly. But we do talk and we know when families need something, or when staff is moving on. We know how to connect people so that families and staff are the happiest."

This is too good to be true. The thought of trying to find

a nanny while handling a newborn and waiting for Alex to get back from Europe is too much, but if Mary can really help me then I can be the mom I wanted to be, even if I have a little extra help around the house.

"So you're telling me you know a nanny?"

"I do. Her name is Jenna."

As soon as the woman's name is out of Mary's mouth, I feel my stomach twist and I start shaking my head before she has a chance to continue. "No, not Jenna. Besides, she's pregnant."

Mary frowns. "What are you talking about?"

Hesitating, I try to decide if I can come clean about looking at Alex's emails and seeing the ultrasounds from Jenna. I don't feel entirely comfortable about it.

"I just know a Jenna who's pregnant," I lie. "I didn't know if you meant the same woman."

This makes Mary laugh and the sound fills the kitchen, causing me to relax. The more I've gotten to know Mary, the more I like her. She's kind, quick to think of other people, and willing to do whatever it takes to help out.

It's strange for me to feel this growing connection with Mary, but how many times have I heard that stress or a major shared experience will make you feel closer to someone?

"You don't have to worry, Katie," Mary says, pulling me in for a hug. "I love you and Alex and I wouldn't do anything that would be anything but the best for your baby. The Jenna I know, she's amazing. She's motivated, good with kids, patient, kind. I think she'd be a great fit for the family."

"Okay, I want to meet her," I say, stepping back from her. "I'd like to make sure she's going to be a good fit. Do you think she'd be open to that?"

Mary nods. "Yeah, she'd love to meet you, I can almost

guarantee it. But she's out of town for a few weeks, so it will have to be after you have Anna here. I'll talk to her this afternoon and make sure she's on board."

"Thank you." Tears spring to my eyes. Knowing that someone is willing to do whatever it takes to get me all the help I need to be the best mom possible is the best feeling in the world.

I trust Mary.

And I trust Jenna.

This Jenna. Not Alex's Jenna.

Even though I haven't met the woman yet, I know she going to be exactly what our family needs.

24

ALEX

OCTOBER 11

The first four weeks in Europe fly by. I'm used to traveling for work and leaving Katie behind, but traveling while she's pregnant is new to me and not something I'm really keen on.

But it's not like I had a choice. I'm the face of Stanfield Investments now. Ever since my father died, it's been my mother who's in charge, but she thought the clients would like to think it was still a man running the show. The reality is, until I have an heir, I'm just her employee that she could fire at a moment's notice.

This baby will change all of that. As soon as I get the call from Katie that we're finally parents then the company will be mine, the money will be mine, and my family will be set for life.

My mother will remain on the payroll as an advisor, of course, but we both know how much advising she's going to be doing. She's much more interested in traveling than sitting in on *stuffy board meetings*.

Her words, not mine.

Still, the only words that really matter are the ones in

clause 7 of my late father's Will, the ones making it clear that I have to have an heir for the company pass to me. Otherwise, if I'm still childless upon my mother's death, it will be dissolved, sold to shareholders, completely broken up, and Katie and I will have nothing.

The anxiety of worrying about my wife in labor when I am on another continent has me in the hotel bar. It's fancy, a thick wooden slab with gold engraving on the edges, and I'm seated on a green leather stool that's perfectly worn in and comfortable.

From here I can swivel around and look at the rest of the bar and restaurant, but I keep my eyes straight ahead, my phone out in front of me, willing it to ring.

She promised me she'd call as soon as she had the baby. When she went into labor she sent a text but that hadn't been enough for me. I'd called her back right away. She'd been breathless on the phone.

The contractions weren't too painful, she said.

She couldn't wait to meet Anna, she said.

I can't either.

Even the knowledge that my wife is in labor makes it impossible for me to push Jenna from my mind. Supposedly, she's already a mom. I kept tabs on Jenna's due date, and I'm already a father. Although Jenna's baby doesn't matter, not really.

Katie's and my daughter does.

I don't even know if Jenna had a boy or a girl, and I'm not interested in finding out. What would be the use anyway? The two of us had a lot of fun, but that time is over.

Still, it's strange knowing that Jenna's child and Anna will be so close in age. They might be in the same class at school—

That thought makes me finish my whiskey in one enormous swallow. I can't imagine having to see Jenna on a regular basis, having to have play dates with her and her child, knowing full well that it's also mine.

"Another whiskey, sir?" The bartender appears in front of me, a towel over his shoulder, a tired expression on his face. The bar isn't busy enough to keep him hopping, so I'm sure it's not that he's being worked too hard that's making him look so tired.

"Do you have children?" The question is out of my mouth before I realize I'm going to ask it and he looks surprised.

"Yeah, twins. They're three and quite a handful." He smiles. "What about you? Kids?"

"One on the way right now," I say. "Anna. My wife is back in the United States and I'm here, but what can you do?"

"Is this your first?" The waiter grabs the bottle of whiskey and pours me a glass, sliding it across the bar to me. "The first is always pretty incredible."

"My first, yeah." The lie feels thick in my throat, like oil, but there's no way this man will ever know the truth.

No one will ever know the truth.

"Well, congrats. This one's on me," he says, pointing to the glass. "Hopefully you get some good news soon."

"Thanks." Lifting the glass, I hold it up to him in a toast. "Here's to being a dad."

I'm just swallowing the last of the whiskey when my phone rings. My fingers suddenly feel fat, like they don't want to work the way they're supposed to, but I manage to pick it up from the bar and swipe it on.

Katie.

"How are you?" I manage to ask. "And how is Anna?"

"She's perfect." Katie sounds calm. Maybe a little tired. When I close my eyes I can just imagine the hospital room, imagine her hooked up to the monitors and machines, but none of that matters, not now that we finally have our perfect little girl.

"And what about you? Are you in a lot of pain?"

When she laughs I feel myself relax and I lean on the bar, catching the eye of the bartender. He raises his eyebrows in question and I give him a thumbs-up to let him know that everything is okay.

"I feel great. I went with the epidural, like we decided, and everything just went smooth as silk. I'll be back home tomorrow."

"I love you," I tell her. "Can you send a picture?"

"You got it. I'll send you one now." The sudden sound of crying almost drowns her out. "I gotta go, our daughter's hungry. I'm trying to get her to latch but she doesn't want to so I'm just going to go with formula."

I don't love the idea of formula, but who am I to tell Katie what she can and can't do? "Whatever you think is best," I tell her. "You're the best mom ever."

She hangs up and I hold my phone in my hand, waiting as patiently as I can for the picture to come through.

It takes a few moments, but then there they are, my wife and my daughter, Katie turned to the camera, Anna already with a bottle in her mouth. She's perfect, with fluffy dark hair and full cheeks. Some newborns look lumpy and misshapen, but not my girl. She's beautiful.

Tapping on the picture, I save it, then set it as my background.

There. Now I can look at the two of them all day long.

I'm about to shut off my phone when something catches my eye.

I've been in hospitals before. I've broken bones as a child, and needed IVs when I was very sick with the flu.

The walls are always the same. All of them beige, off-white, almost a sickly green undertone. What I'm seeing right now just doesn't make any sense.

It's a tiny sliver of wall behind Katie's head that's buttercup yellow.

25

KATIE

I send Alex the picture of Anna and me without really thinking about what we look like, then put my phone down on the small table by the rocker and snuggle her up to my chest.

She's perfect. It's been almost impossible for me to keep myself from telling Alex all about her up until now, especially since I've had her for almost two weeks, but I had to wait.

Otherwise I'd have had to have told him that she was a bit of a preemie, and he'd have been on the first flight back to the US. I simply can't have that.

"Your daddy is going to love you," I coo to her, stroking her cheek as she drinks. Her little hands are balled up into tight fists and she wiggles a bit against me, doing everything she can to get the last bit of formula from the bottle.

I know Alex isn't going to be thrilled about the fact that Anna isn't going to be breastfed, but he's just going to have to get over it.

Even if I wanted to breastfeed, I couldn't.

The soft knock on the door makes me look up. Mary's standing there, a woman I've never seen before next to her. The younger woman has long dark hair in a braid down her back and smiles at me before looking down at the baby in my arms and smiling even more.

"Katie, this is Jenna," Mary says, and gently pushes the younger woman into the room. "She's finally back from vacation and I know you were interested in meeting her."

"Oh, wonderful," I say, standing up. I move slowly, to make it look like I really gave birth. I think I'm pretty convincing. Mary is the only person who can ever know the truth, and although she trusts this nanny enough to suggest that we hire her, I don't know the woman and I'm not going to confide in her about this.

Not now. Not ever.

"Look at your sweet little girl," Jenna coos, reaching out and lightly touching Anna's head. "She's just gorgeous, Katie."

I stiffen. I'm not sure why, but there's something about how the woman reaches out and touches Anna without first asking permission that rubs me the wrong way. Then I tell myself to relax.

She's a nanny. Nannies like kids. She's going to want to reach out and meet my daughter.

"Thank you," I finally manage to say. "I can't wait for her daddy to meet her so we can talk about who we think she looks like more. She has my nose, don't you think?"

Mary smiles and Jenna laughs. "She really does." Even though she's laughing, I catch a small frown on her face, but I ignore it.

She spends her life taking care of other people's children. It makes sense that she might be a little sad not to have one of her own yet. Didn't Mary say that was the case?

"Why don't we all sit and we can talk about what kind of help I think I'm going to need," I say, gesturing to the seats around us. At that moment Anna starts to fuss, turning her head side to side like she's hungry. "Oh, hang on, she needs a bottle. I have one on the coffee table, if you'll just give me a minute."

"I'll take care of it." Like a seasoned pro, Jenna flips a cloth up over her shoulder and grabs the bottle, taking Anna from me before I even realize what's going on. "Sit, Katie. I'm more than happy to take her and feed her while we talk."

Anna quiets right down. Not only does she find the bottle immediately, but she turns her little face in to Jenna, her entire body seeming to relax as she eats.

"She calmed right down," I say, unable to keep the wonder out of my voice.

Jenna looks at me. "Is that not normal? Is she a fussy baby?"

"I don't think she's any fussier than other babies," I say cautiously. I'm not sure why, but there's a part of me that doesn't like what Jenna just said. Before I can decide if I'm offended or overreacting, she smiles and speaks.

"Oh, sorry, I didn't mean to imply that you were doing anything wrong, Katie. Some babies fuss more than others, that's all. It's probably just that she's enjoying someone else holding her for a change. Babies sometimes need new stimulation to calm down."

That was definitely not mentioned in any of the parenting books I read, but I smile at Jenna in appreciation. It's a relief to have someone here to help who really cares and is so good with kids, and knows what she's doing. Without her, well, I don't know where I'd be.

Wow, I'm relying on her and I haven't even hired her yet.

"So tell me what you're looking for in a nanny," Jenna says, dragging her eyes away from Anna's sweet face to look at me. "Mary tells me you have your hands full a lot of the time with commitments outside the home. I can be here as much or as little as you want."

"I do volunteer a lot," I say, twisting my hands together before I catch what I'm doing and stop myself. "It's thanks to my husband's job. He needs me out there all the time being the face of his company at social events."

"Sounds like he might not be home all the time. That has to be so hard." Jenna's voice is sympathetic and kind, and even though I don't love what she just said, I can't be mad at her, and I shake my head.

"Yeah. He works really long hours and then often has meetings at night. Sometimes he'll leave in the morning and I won't see him again until he's falling into bed after I've been asleep for a while. It's not always easy, but he's a good man."

"I'm sure he is. Where is he right now?" Jenna puts the empty bottle on the coffee table between us and lifts Anna to her shoulder, gently rubbing her back.

"Europe," I say, and even though I haven't really been emotional about him being gone, I suddenly feel a little sad.

"He wasn't here when Anna was born," Mary says, reaching over to me and taking me by the hand. "But Katie was a champ and got through it no problem."

"Well, you seem to have everything under control," Jenna tells me, snuggling Anna against her chest and leaning down to kiss her forehead. "But I'd love to come and spend time with you two and help. You'll be able to rest without worrying about keeping one ear open for any cries, you'll be able to get out into the community to do what needs to be done. I'd offer to help with laundry and picking up the house as well, but you have Mary for that."

She's grinning at me and I can't help but smile back. "Sounds amazing. You're hired," I tell her, standing and reaching for Anna. It's been long enough without my baby in my arms and I want her back.

For a moment, I think Jenna hesitates before handing her over, but I must be imagining things. What kind of a nanny would she be if she was like that?

"Wonderful. How about this," Jenna says, stretching and glancing at her watch. "You look like you need a nap, and I could use some time getting to know little Anna here. Why don't you go rest and I'll take care of her? Mary can show me around so I know where everything is, and by the time you get back up, she and I will have connected and you'll be feeling refreshed."

"How did you know I'm so tired?" I ask, laughing. It's strange to hand Anna back over, but I do after I kiss her sweet little forehead. Jenna tucks her right against her chest and I feel a momentary flutter in my own as I watch my baby being held by another woman.

"You're a new mom," Jenna tells me, grinning. "Not only did you spend nine months growing this sweet little girl, but then you gave birth to her. For bonus points, her dad isn't even around right now. Let me help you, Katie. This is what I'm here for."

"I had no idea I really needed a nanny until Mary convinced me," I tell her. "Seriously, this is amazing. Thank you. I'll be down in a bit." Turning, I start across the living room, finally feeling like I have a handle on things.

This was all I needed. I had no idea how difficult it would be to care for an infant.

Only now I don't have to do it alone any longer.

Jenna is perfect. She's everything. She's going to make sure I'm the best mom possible.

26

ALEX

I'm a little disappointed that Katie doesn't greet me at the door when I get home from Europe, but not really surprised. She couldn't possibly hear me pull up with the loud music pumping through the house.

It's far too loud for someone to play with a sleeping baby, and that tells me that Anna must be up. Excitement courses through my body when I think about meeting my baby girl for the first time. She's my heir, and that's important, but she's more than just that.

She's my daughter, our child, the thing Katie has wanted more than anything since I met her.

Never mind that I have another child out there somewhere.

Leaving my suitcase on the porch, I walk into the foyer and hang my keys up before slowly making my way down the hall to the kitchen, where the music is coming from, with the balloons and flowers I picked up from the grocery store on my way home. I pause for a moment before pushing open the door to take in the scene.

Katie's blasting music from a bluetooth speaker on the counter, wearing her favorite frilled apron, and something that smells delicious is bubbling away on the stove. She turns as I walk in, using a wooden spoon as a microphone, then leans down close to the baby swing on the floor, singing her heart out along with Dolly Parton.

I take a step into the kitchen and Katie looks up. God, she's beautiful. She's absolutely radiant, her smile stretching from ear to ear. She looks just as happy right now as she did when we got married and I hurry to her, meeting her halfway in the kitchen then pulling her into my arms.

"I missed you," I tell her, kissing her on the top of her head as she buries into my chest. "Oh, Katie, I missed you and Anna so much."

"You have to meet her!" Katie pulls away from me, a huge smile on her face. "Alex, you're going to love her. She's so darling, so sweet and perfect. Let me get her."

I wait as Katie hurries to the swing and bends down, cooing to our daughter as she lifts her out and brings her up to her chest.

"Isn't she gorgeous?" Katie says, lightly touching Anna's nose. Anna, in response, screws up her face and holds her fists out from her body. "Do you want to hold her?"

Something's wrong. She's bigger than I thought she would be, for one thing.

For another, it's not that Anna's not beautiful, with pouty little lips and a nose that juts up right at the tip, and dark blue eyes that match her dark hair. No, it's the way she's studying me, with an expression I know all too well.

It's not one of Katie's.

"Alex, what is it?" Katie finally drags her gaze away from Anna's face and looks up at me. "You're being so quiet. What's going on? Don't you want to hold her? She's perfect."

"How old is she?" I choke out the words, moving my arms on autopilot as I let Katie snuggle our daughter into my arms. There's a flash of happiness when Anna looks up at me and purses her lips, but it disappears when I look away to Katie, waiting for her to respond.

"Almost four weeks. Why? You remember when I called." She chuckles, sounding nervous, then spins away from me to hurry back to the stove. "Hold on, I don't want this to burn," she calls over her shoulder and I just let her go.

What else can I do?

For a moment, I just watch her, busy at the stove now, stirring and tasting, noting how happy she looks.

She seems less on edge that she did before I left, when she was still pregnant. I've never heard of any new mom looking and feeling this good before, but everything seems to be working out for her.

Maybe I'm reading everything wrong.

Maybe I'm just tired from my flight.

Maybe this is all in my head.

And then it hits me — why I feel the way I do, and why I keep looking at Anna and thinking that I see someone else in my arms.

I've never seen Jenna's baby.

We're no longer in contact, which is a good thing, but it means I haven't met our child, and possibly never will. The only reason I have even the tiniest feeling that Anna looks more like Jenna than Katie is that I'm so curious what Jenna's baby looks like.

Plus I'm tired, so I'm seeing things that aren't there. I need to just get some rest, enjoy my time with my wife and daughter, and then everything will be better in the morning.

Katie looks so happy, so utterly at peace with being a mom, and I want to feel the same way about being a dad.

That's it. I want to be a great dad.

I can't be that for Jenna's baby, but I can for Katie's, and that's what matters.

27

KATIE

Alex went right back to work this morning. Honestly, I had hoped he would take some time off to spend with Anna and me, but he told me he needed to get back to the office right away so he could make sure he didn't miss any emails from his new European contacts. Also he said that he needed to be around to handle any fires that might break out.

I resisted reminding him that he could check his email from home, and there weren't any fires while he was away, because Alex doesn't like talk like that. He doesn't like to think that the office can function without him there to keep an eye on it. He's super involved with everything, which is part of the reason why Stanfield Investments does such a good business.

Still, I'm not thrilled about him going back to the office. I have all of his laundry to do and I need to go grocery shopping because I just ran out of time to do that yesterday and it would have been great to have his help around the house. And everything is just a little bit different now, thanks to Anna.

Anna.

Between feedings and diaper changes she had me up three times last night, and I'm already looking forward to the nap I'll get when Jenna comes over to watch her. I haven't told Alex that I've hired a nanny because I'm pretty sure he wanted to be involved in the process and the decision.

Unfortunately for him, that decision needed to be made, and quickly, and he wasn't here, so I just went ahead and did it on my own. I don't really think he'll be mad, but I'm sure he'll want to know how I vetted her and how I decided she was a good candidate.

That's why I had her write down a list of all of her qualifications yesterday before she left for the evening. She really does look great on paper, and I can already attest to how amazing she is in person. Most importantly, Anna loves her, much more than I would have thought she would a nanny.

It's almost like the two of them have some sort of a connection already. Then again, I've always believed in the idea of soul mates — not just your romantic partner, but also other people you may run into during your life. It's quite possible that Anna and Jenna were meant to have some sort of a connection.

Whatever it is, I love how my daughter stops crying whenever Jenna picks her up, how she reaches for her when I hand her over, how willing Jenna is to handle any dirty diapers that I don't feel like changing at that moment.

Right now I'm standing in the foyer, Anna in my arms, my purse over my shoulder, ready to go as soon as Jenna gets here. I feel great, if a little tired, and I have to admit that not dealing with breastfeeding or anything else that happens to your body after giving birth is fantastic.

Alex kept commenting on how healthy and happy I

looked last night, and I couldn't help but smile. He is still my husband, after all, and I'm glad I don't have to worry about him not wanting me anymore after giving birth. I've heard some new moms struggle with that.

I'm about to check my watch to see where Jenna might be when I hear both Jenna and Mary on the porch. I'm thrilled that they're here at the same time so they can start taking care of things around the house.

"Good morning!" I say, throwing open the front door and moving out of the way for the two of them to come in. "We're so happy to see you, aren't we, Anna?" I lean down and kiss my daughter before Jenna takes her, gently pressing a kiss against her forehead as well.

"Hello, my baby," Jenna says, and I pause.

Her baby?

Does she call her that often?

Mary laughs, obviously seeing the look on my face. "You've never heard nannies say that? Oh, they do it all the time. It's the best way to really form a connection with the child, isn't it?"

Jenna nods, her cheeks flushed. "Yeah, I'm sorry. I'm so used to doing that. I hope it didn't upset you."

"Of course not." I smile, forcing myself to calm down. "It took me by surprise, that's all, but you're so good with her, who I am I tell you what you should call her? You two seem like you've known each other for years."

"Funny, because she's only about six weeks old." Jenna grins at Anna.

I shake my head. "Four weeks." I have to keep my story straight and make sure that everyone is on the same page with what I'm calling Anna's birthdate.

I know she's a bit older than I'm telling Alex, but that

was the only way to make sure he didn't worry about her being a preemie.

As it is, I've had to deflect his mother every chance I can.

"Right, four weeks, I'm sorry. She's just so big and smart and beautiful that I forgot for a minute how brand new she is." Jenna gives me a smile and I feel myself relax. "Will you be gone all day? I was thinking I'd take her to the park."

"Yeah, it's going to be a busy one." I feel a pang at leaving Anna with the nanny all day long. That's something I didn't think I would do so soon, but I really do have a lot to do and I'm not sure how else I'm going to accomplish everything.

Not only do I have errands to run, but there's a team of guys coming to start work on the roof today. It's going to be crazy around here, and while I know it's probably terrible of me to think it, I'm glad I won't be the one trying to get Anna down for a nap while they're banging away. "If you guys do go to the park just send me a text so I know, okay? I want to know where she is."

"Not a problem. We're happy to do that." Jenna takes Anna's little fist in her hand and waves it at me. "Have fun, Momma! We'll be good girls."

Even though I have no doubt in my mind that everything is going to be okay, there's still a strange pit in my stomach when I wave goodbye to the three of them and finally turn to go to the garage. It's one thing to be in the house all day when Jenna is with Anna keeping an eye on her, but another entirely to leave them alone and hope that everything will be fine.

"You're just nervous. It's normal new mom stuff," I mutter to myself, hurrying to my car and pushing the button above my head to open the garage door. "Everything is going to be fine. They're going to go to the park, you're going to run errands, and when Alex gets home tonight he'll totally understand when you tell him you hired a nanny."

He'll get it, won't he? There's no reason to think that he won't.

He's always supported me in everything else I do.

Why wouldn't he now?

28

ALEX

At work, it's hard for me to keep my mind on what I'm doing. I know Katie wanted me to be home with her and Anna today.

I always do my best to handle everything at work myself so I know it's done correctly, but because I was only attending to the most pressing emails while I was away so I would have more time for face to face meetings, my inbox is stuffed full of messages I need to sort through now and I groan, leaning back in my chair, forcing myself to click the first of way too many. Most of it is junk, or ancient history, but that doesn't mean I can do a mass delete, no matter how much I'd like to. There might be something of value in here, something I need to know about or keep an eye on, and that means I need to go through every single email, no matter how time consuming it may be and no matter how badly it makes me want to pour myself a drink.

I make myself a deal. I'll take care of the first fifty emails and then text Katie to see what she and Anna are up to. I bet they're doing something fun and maybe I can live vicariously through them.

That thought spurring me on, I work studiously for the next forty-five minutes, then fire off a text to my wife asking what she's up to and for a picture of Anna.

Then I wait.

Drumming my fingers, I sit back in my chair. Where is she? Normally Katie responds to my texts immediately, but maybe she and Anna are distracted or caught up with something. Still, it's a little strange that she doesn't text me right back.

I'm about to pick up my phone and call her when it vibrates and I tap the screen, greedy for a picture of my baby. "Awww, at the park," I whisper, tapping the picture she sent. There's my sweet baby, her eyes closed, her head turned to the side. Her mouth has opened slightly in sleep.

She's nestled in that ridiculously expensive stroller Katie wanted. I told her I didn't really think we needed something that came with side air bags, but I'm admittedly a little impressed with it now that we have it.

I'm about to put my phone down when I look closer at the screen, then zoom in to look behind the stroller.

They're at the park right by the office.

I get up from my desk and hurry to the window overlooking that part of town. I can see the park from here, see the giant play structure that, during the summer, is teeming with children. How many hours have I stood here and stared outside when I had something on my mind? I'd recognize that park anywhere.

Looks like you're having fun.

I don't want to tell her I'm coming to see them. It will be a great surprise if I just show up at the park. I know she hated that I had to go into the office this morning. Hopefully this will show her that I've been thinking about them the entire time. Grabbing my jacket from the back of my chair, I hurry out of the office, keeping my head down so nobody will talk to me.

We're having a blast! Miss you though.

Katie's text comes through as I'm crossing the street. The park is just three blocks away and I walk quickly, holding my jacket tight around me against the breeze. It's a surprisingly warm day here today and the sun feels really good on my face. I'd be worried about Anna being out in the wind but she certainly looked cozy enough all bundled up like a little burrito.

Excitement courses through me. How long has it been since I left the office like this just because I wanted to? I'm filled with the desire to see my little family and I walk faster, ignoring other people doing the same. We're all in a hurry wanting to get to wherever it is we're going.

At the park I have to slow down, though, to wait for a preschool class to be led out. They're all holding onto bright colorful rings that are attached to a long strap. One teacher is in the front and there's another one in the back to make sure no kids get lost on the way back to class.

They're all laughing except for one little boy who has a scraped knee and a tearstained face and I give him a sympathetic smile as he walks by.

What can I say? Becoming a dad has turned me into a softie.

"Okay, darlings, where are you?" I mutter to myself. Checking the picture Katie sent me, I orient myself in the park, trying to figure out exactly where she and Anna must be sitting. The park is huge, sprawling, with lots of paths in every direction, and I pick one, walking with purpose as I check my phone from time to time to make sure I'm headed in the right direction.

I'm pretty sure I am. My office is to the left, and when I

turn a little I see the same view I saw in the picture. Now I just have to find my wife.

Craning my neck, I step around a sweet little old couple holding hands on their stroll and a man with three dogs all walking patiently at his side. Somewhere there's a child crying, but I don't think it's Anna.

"Where are you?" I mutter again. As hard as I look, I'm not seeing my wife's blonde hair, or her coat. She has a bright pink jacket she loves to wear in this type of weather and usually it's like a beacon, making it easy for me to find her anywhere in a crowd.

Finally I give up and text her.

Where are you? I'm at the park.

Even though I hate to ruin the surprise, it doesn't look like I'm going to find her otherwise. She could be anywhere.

You're at the park?? We left already, I'm so sorry!

My shoulders slump. It was silly to think I could nip out of work and see the two of them during the middle of my day, but I really liked the idea.

Not a problem. Some other time. See you at home. Love you.

I try to see the bright side as I turn to walk back through the park to my office. Even though I didn't get to see my girls, it was a nice day to be outside and stretching my legs a little bit is good for me. Hopefully Katie will think it was sweet of me to come looking for her like this. I know she really didn't want me to go to work today, any more than she wanted me to be in Europe when Anna was born, but I didn't have a choice. I hope she understands that.

I'll let you know the next time I come there so we can plan. Love you too!

Sighing, I slip my phone back into my pocket and look around me on the off chance that she might still be here, even though I know she's not, she just told me that she's not. Hey, a guy can hope, can't he?

My eyes land on the bench where she must have been sitting. It's definitely the one, with my building in the background, but there isn't a blonde in a hot pink jacket with a stroller sitting there.

There is a woman with a stroller, though. She has thick dark hair that falls around her face as she peers into the stroller, obviously talking to the baby inside.

I'd know that woman anywhere.

Then I look again and what I see doesn't make any sense.

I'd also know that stroller anywhere.

29

KATIE

Panic shoots through my body when Alex texts that he went looking for me at the park. What if he runs into Jenna with Anna? I need to tell him about the nanny, should have told him last night, but we were busy spending quality time together, and honestly, the last thing I wanted to do was bring up another woman.

Especially one who has the same name as the woman sending him ultrasounds.

I never should have asked Jenna to send me a picture of what she and Anna were doing. Well, that part was probably okay, but then sending it on to Alex like he wouldn't get curious about what park we were at?

Big mistake. I won't do that again.

At the time, I hadn't paid attention to which park Jenna took Anna to, but now that I think about it, that park is way across town. There are two parks closer to home, and although that one is the best one for kids to go play, it's not like Anna is getting out of her stroller and running to the sand pit anytime soon.

So why did she take her there?

I'm still fretting about that as I pull into the garage and park the car. The trunk is loaded with groceries and I know I shouldn't leave them in there but I want to talk to Mary right away. Her car is gone from the driveway, but that's probably just because Jenna took Anna to the park.

Mary told me the two of them would carpool from time to time and not to worry if I only saw one car in the driveway, or if there wasn't a car there at all.

Ignoring the steak in the trunk, I let myself into the house, then pause to listen. I can hear her moving around in the kitchen.

"Katie, hi!" Mary looks up as I walk into the room. She's up to her elbows in soapy water in the sink but turns off the faucet to talk to me. "How were the errands? You all done for the day?"

"Yep." I pop the *p,* feeling self-conscious. I have no idea how to broach this topic but I know I need to go ahead and do it. "Hey, I have a question about Jenna."

Her expression changes, grows concerned. "Is everything okay?" She'd been busy a moment ago but now it feels like I have one hundred percent of her attention.

"Oh, sure, nothing's wrong." I manage to plaster a smile on my face even though I feel like I could throw up. "She's amazing, seriously. I don't think I've ever met anyone like her."

"She's certainly great with kids," Mary tells me, nodding as she wipes her hands on a towel which she then tosses onto the counter. "I've known her for years and she's always been really passionate about working with them."

"Does she have any herself? I couldn't remember if you told me." I try to sound as casual as possible even though I have a very good feeling Mary can tell how on edge I am. I honestly feel like I'm going to come out of my skin.

"Jenna? Kids?" Mary frowns and looks up for a second like she's trying to think, then shakes her head. "Nope. She talked about having kids a while back but I guess it just never worked out. Why do you ask?"

There's no way I can tell Mary about snooping through Alex's emails and finding one from a woman named Jenna, a woman who was clearly pregnant and wanted to tell Alex about it. Meanwhile Mary is telling me that the Jenna who works for me hasn't ever had kids.

I don't have a reason not to believe her.

And yet . . .

I can't shake the question that has been eating at me since I found the email from Jenna, can't stop wondering why she would go out of her way to let Alex know she was pregnant unless she knew there was a good reason for her to do so.

Unless she knew he would take a personal interest in the baby.

He wouldn't have another baby. I know he wouldn't.

"I just know another Jenna who had a baby around this time and thought it a little weird, that's all. I mean, how many Jennas are there in Tennessee?"

"I think it's a pretty common name these days," Mary says, eyeballing me. "I guess it's just a weird coincidence. Did I ever tell you, I was named Mary for a friend my mom had when she was in high school. They hadn't seen each other in years, and then guess who was the nurse working the maternity ward the night I was born?"

"Let me guess. Mary?" I say, trying to sound interested. I'm not. I'm thinking about what it might mean if this Jenna and the Jenna emailing Alex are the same woman.

No matter how many times I try to turn that over in my head to make it make sense, I simply can't.

They're not the same woman. There's no way on earth they are.

"Anyway, Katie," Mary says, turning back to the sink and talking to me over her shoulder, "if there's nothing else you really need right now then I'm going to get back to work. Plenty to do, you know. Babies make a lot of empty bottles and as soon as Jenna and little Anna get back from the park I'm going to have a lot to wash."

"No, that's fine," I say, getting the very distinct sense I was just dismissed from the room. It's a strange feeling to have, especially when I'm the one who pays Mary's wages.

But I leave the kitchen meekly, turning and walking to the front of the house to look out the window. Surely Alex will be home soon.

I start to feel a little nervous. Sure, having the day to myself and not having to worry about Anna fussing when I've been out running errands has been nice. I even managed to finish everything on my to-do list early and rewarded myself with a little trip to get a massage and pedicure. I feel like a real person, not just a tired mom, and I have to admit that it's nice.

But where is my husband?

And Jenna?

And, perhaps more importantly, where is my baby?

A line of sweat trickles its way down my back and I shift position nervously as I stand at the window. Yes, I trust Mary, but I don't really know Jenna, do I?

I just opened my doors to her, let her waltz right into my house, and allowed her to spend time with my daughter.

Worse than that.

I let her *take* my daughter from the house.

Sweat breaks out on my brow and I grip the window

frame, my nails pressing into the wood as I stare outside and will Mary's car to appear.

That's the only saving grace I have right now. Mary's still here, which means Jenna has to come back with Anna to pick up her friend.

I start to relax when I see a car turn into the driveway.

Except there's just one problem.

It's not Jenna coming home.

It's Alex.

30

ALEX

I don't want to admit to myself how much seeing Jenna at the park rattled me.

I knew it was her, knew it from the moment she turned and I saw the soft cheek I have cupped in my hand so many times, knew it from the moment she lightly reached down into the stroller to touch the baby inside.

A stroller that looks exactly like the one we have.

It's a staggering coincidence, and I don't usually believe in those.

I don't *ever* believe in those.

As I drive home from the office, I keep squeezing the steering wheel as hard as I can, then slowly letting it go again. I need to do something — anything — to prevent the uncomfortable thought growing at the back of my mind from really taking root.

That's why I'm leaving work early.

I told Emma that I wasn't feeling very well and that I needed to go home and rest. She assumed it's jetlag, and I wasn't about to correct her.

How in the world could I tell her that the real problem was that I saw my former mistress at the park with a baby?

With our baby?

I press down harder on the gas, shaking my head to try to clear the thoughts that are tumbling around each other inside and making it impossible for me to think straight.

"That might not have been Jenna at the park," I whisper. "It really might not have been."

No.

The woman at the park was Jenna. I'd know her anywhere, know the gorgeous smile she has when she's happy, know the gentle way her eyes crinkle when she's thinking hard about something. I can try to tell myself that it wasn't Jenna at the park all I like, but that's a lie.

So then I think about the stroller, trying to make that puzzle piece make sense. If it was Jenna at the park, *which it was*, then how weird would it be for her to have the same stroller as Katie chose?

Unless she wasn't with her own baby.

Unless she was with ours.

But why would she be? An in that case, what happened to hers?

"Dammit, none of this makes any sense," I mutter, finally pulling into the driveway. I don't even bother parking in the garage, instead I hop out and hurry up to the front porch, my house key already ready in my hand.

Before I can insert my key, the door opens and Katie flies past me, a tight expression on her face, then hurries to the driveway to meet a woman who's pulling up in a Camry. Before the woman can get out to open the back door of the car, Katie does, then leans in and pulls out a car seat, looping her arm through the handle and slamming the door.

The driver has her back to me, but I see the long thick braid.

Then I see her profile as she turns to my wife.

"I'll be back tomorrow, Katie! I hope you had a great day. Little Anna was a dream at the park and I think we'll probably start going there more often. I know she's too little to play, but she loved looking at everything as people walked by." Then a laugh, the sound of it racing up and down my spine.

Jenna.

I could pick that voice and laugh out of a crowded room with the lights off and other people talking. There's no way to make sense of it, but Jenna is standing in my driveway, my wife and daughter at her car.

And not a single one of them looks upset.

Scratch that.

Katie does.

I don't even realize I'm walking down the porch stairs until I'm standing on the driveway with the women, and I can't help the words that fly out of my mouth when Jenna's eyes land on mine.

"What are you doing here?" There's no venom in my voice, only shock.

Katie pushes past Jenna, holding the car seat in front of her like a weapon. Anna is awake, her big blue eyes blinking hard at the bright light outside.

"Alex, you're home early! What perfect timing. I was going to tell you tonight, I hired a nanny. I'd like you to meet Jenna."

A nanny.

"It's a pleasure," Jenna says, and then her hand is extended toward mine. I hesitate just a moment before reaching out and taking it. It's cool, her skin soft, just like it always was.

Do I hold her hand too long? Is the smile on her face because she knows that my mind is working overtime and I can't figure out what's really going on? Is Katie going to notice that something's wrong?

I pull my hand back and look down at my child, then slowly bring my eyes back up to Jenna.

It can't be.

"So nice to meet you," I say, choosing my words carefully. "I'm sure you've been a great help to my wife while she's been recovering from giving birth. It's hard on the body."

"It is." She nods, like this is a totally normal conversation for two people to be having, like she's meeting me for the first time. "But Katie is a champ. You'd never even know she's just had a baby, she's up and at it, on her feet, no complaining. Not like some women I know."

Katie squeaks and when I look at her, her eyes are wide as she stares at Jenna. I'm not sure what's going through her mind right now, but I honestly don't care. What matters to me is finding out what Jenna is doing in my house and what game she thinks she's playing.

And then it hits me.

I don't know why I didn't notice it earlier. Moving carefully, I bend down and get Anna out of her car seat. At first, I don't think my wife is going to give her up, but then she does, putting the car seat on the ground so I can pull Anna free. She's whimpering a little and I snuggle my baby against my chest, cooing at her as I really drink in her face.

She's too old. She's not the newborn Katie said she was.

I think about the picture she sent me when Anna was just born

(when she said Anna was just born)

and how it didn't make any sense.

I look at Anna's face, at her nose, at the shape of her eyes.

And then I look right back up at her mother. Her real mother.

Jenna doesn't flinch.

"I can't wait to hear about your qualifications," I tell her, kissing my daughter on the forehead. She's not Katie's, that much is painfully obvious now that I really look at her, but she's still mine. She's still my little girl, still the heir I need.

I just don't know how the hell any of this came to be.

"I'd love to sit down with you sometime, and you can interview past families I've worked for as well," Jenna tells me. "But right now I'm afraid Mary and I need to go. She's my ride, and she has something she has to do tonight."

"Of course. Well, it's a pleasure to meet you, Jenna. Thanks for taking such good care of our baby."

Our baby.

Will she pick up on that and know that I've guessed the truth?

Her eyes narrow, just a bit. Not enough that I think Mary or Katie will notice, but I do.

"You made a beautiful child," Jenna says, turning to Katie and giving her a small wave. "Thanks for letting me be a small part of her life."

"Thank you." Katie's cheeks are flushed and she loops her arm around my waist, snuggling close to me like she's unsure of where the two of us stand. "I'll see you both in the morning!"

Mary and Jenna leave Katie and I are left standing on the driveway, watching Mary and Jenna go. Anna doesn't stir. She's a happy baby, more relaxed than most infants I've heard the horror stories about. I nuzzle her gently before turning to the house and gesturing for Katie to lead us in.

"Why don't we go on in and you can tell me everything you know about this new nanny?"

I've never wanted to think my wife was lying to me.

But right now I can't wait to hear what fairy tales she comes up with.

31

KATIE

There's a buzzing in the back of my mind when Alex and I walk into the kitchen, Anna in his arms, my hands twisting in front of my body as I lead the way.

It's soft, barely noticeable, but still. It's as if a dozen baby bumblebees have taken up residence in my skull.

Alex is not happy about me having a nanny, that's obvious, but I feel there's something more than that going on. I saw the way he and Jenna looked at each other, like they already knew each other and were surprised to run into each other.

I saw the way he stared at Anna, at her sweet little face, then looked back up at the nanny.

None of it sat well with me. It all made me incredibly nervous and even though I'd like to pretend that it didn't happen, it did.

I saw it.

My hands shake a little as I pour us each a glass of wine and then glance at the clock. "You're home early," I say, handing him his drink. He's shifted Anna to rest more on his shoulder, her face turned to the side, and he takes the glass from me with his free hand. "I'm assuming you're probably not hungry yet, am I right?"

"Not really, no. Why don't we go find a place to sit and then the two of us can talk?" His tone is light, but I hear what he's really saying.

Why don't you try to explain exactly why you hired a nanny and didn't tell me about it?

"That sounds great." I follow him to the living room, my heart beating hard. As soon as we're both settled in our chairs, the words start to spill out of me. I can't help it.

"I'm sorry I didn't tell you about Jenna right away," I say, wanting to cut him off before he even gets started. Alex really doesn't like being left in the dark about anything. If I can keep him from finding out just *how* in the dark he is regarding Anna then things are going to work out okay.

I hope.

"I just . . . you are going to be such a good dad, I know that you are, and I want to be just as good a mom, but I was so tired." I lay it on thick, hoping he'll see that I really didn't have a choice. "I did this for us, so that I would have some energy at the end of the day."

"You're always thinking of other people," he tells me, and I stiffen at his words, but then watch him while he takes a sip of his wine.

It wasn't malicious. He sounded sincere, and even though I know I could take it in a very different way, I'm going to assume that he was being kind.

"I just want what's best for this family. For Anna." When he doesn't respond I'm overwhelmed with the desire to fill the silence between us. I've never been very good at sitting quietly and letting other people have time with their thoughts. So I keep talking.

"When Mary told me she knew an incredible nanny that was available, I jumped at the chance to meet her." I want Alex to see why I did what I did, that it wasn't just me making a stupid decision. "We've always said how much we both trust Mary and so I figured that if she had this great person for us to hire then I should definitely give the woman the benefit of the doubt. And I'm so glad I did! You should see Jenna with Anna. The two of them get along so well you'd think—"

I don't want to finish that thought.

Alex does it for me.

"You'd think they were family?" He watches me as he speaks and I nod, swallowing hard. That's one thing about my husband that I've always admired, even if I don't necessarily appreciate it at the time. He's great at getting to the heart of the matter, at figuring out what's really going on.

"You'd think so, yeah." My mouth feels dry. "Jenna adores her, and Anna took to Jenna right away. It was pretty amazing."

I'm saying too much. Even though Alex isn't looking at me right now, I can tell that I'm babbling and I'm going to get myself into trouble if I'm not careful. I drink more wine, slowly tipping the glass up to drain it as I watch him.

He's put his wine down and is rubbing Anna's back. His movements are slow, deliberate, just like everything else that he does. I've never met a man more willing to think things through before making a decision.

It's one of the things I've always loved about him. Where I'll leap before I look, before I even have time to gauge how deep the water is, he will take his time, considering things from all angles, see how different situations could fit together or play out.

Normally, I love that about him.

But right now it's making me very nervous.

He's thinking something, but in true Alex fashion, he's not about to share his thoughts with me until he's ready. I'm going to have to wait, and that's not something I'm great at.

"Alex," I say, when the silence has gotten too oppressive between us, pressing down on me like a wet wool blanket, "please tell me what you're thinking. I want to know if you think I've really messed up."

Slowly, as if it hurts to move his head, he turns to look at me.

"Where's her birth certificate?"

"Do what?" The question is so out of left field that I have to blink at him to try to clear my thoughts. "Her birth certificate?"

He nods and I feel myself grow cold.

That's not something I ever thought about. It never once crossed my mind how in the world we were going to put my name on the birth certificate. I was just so happy to have a baby to replace the one I lost, to have a daughter I could love, to have a child that would ensure Alex kept the family business, that I forgot about that.

How could I have been so stupid?

I tip my wine glass back up to my lips before I remember that it's empty and put it down on my leg, holding it there by the stem to make sure it doesn't tip over and break. Alex is still looking at me, waiting for an answer, and I know I need to come up with something to tell him before he gets upset with me.

"The safe deposit box at the bank." The lie flies out my mouth easily. "I took it there after we got home from the hospital and stashed it so that it would be safe and out of the way. I'm probably paranoid, but can you imagine what would happen if we lost it?"

"That was a good idea," he tells me, and I feel myself relax. "You always think of everything."

That's a laugh. I didn't, not in this case, but it looks like I bought myself a little time at least.

Mary and I have something to talk about tomorrow morning and I'm sure she's going to be surprised. Or maybe she's already figured something out. I hope so. Anna needs a birth certificate or she'll never be able to live a normal life.

Then it hits me. Maybe at some point later I could lie, say that it got lost. There's no reason to get Mary any more involved than she is already.

I'll handle it all on my own.

And Alex will never know.

32

ALEX

I told Katie I wanted to talk to the nanny this morning before I left for work. By making sure I didn't use Jenna's name, I hope that I came across as appropriately clueless as to who the woman watching over our baby really is.

If Katie knew the truth, if she knew about me and Jenna, about the fact that the little girl she holds in her arms every day is my daughter with her nanny, I can't even imagine how she would react.

No, I can't let her know that right now, especially not after she looked me dead in the eye last night and lied to me. She doesn't have the birth certificate for Anna because she's not the mom. She didn't take it to the bank for safekeeping. It doesn't exist.

At least, not with Katie's name on it.

But then how did all of this come about? If Jenna gave birth to Anna, which I'm sure she did, what happened to Katie's baby? And why would Jenna agree to give up her child?

And how did she luck into a nanny position in our house?

I don't think it's luck. That's something I've never believed in, and I'm sure as hell not about to start now. This isn't a series of strange coincidences that's brought us together like this.

Someone is pulling the strings, and I want to know who.

It's still a little dark on the front porch and Mary and Jenna don't see me as they walk up to the house. They carpooled this morning, which is something Katie told me they said they do as often as possible. I'm sitting in a rocking chair, keeping completely still, watching and listening.

What I hear doesn't disappoint.

"You know that I'd do anything for you, darling," Mary says, turning and cupping Jenna's cheek before the two of them knock on the door. I've done that. I've cupped her cheek and told her almost the same thing.

I force myself to stay still, to stay quiet.

"I know, Mom. And I know this is the right thing to do, that I can't raise Anna on my own, but it's hard. Even harder now that Alex is home."

Mary is Jenna's mother?

Of course, we never did the whole meet-the-family thing since we weren't officially together. But holy hell, I never imagined that I was sleeping with the housekeeper's daughter, much less that they might be working together to conspire against me and my wife.

Anger, hot and red, flashes through me and I have to force myself to stay in the rocking chair. It would be so easy to get up now. I can just imagine the look of surprise on Jenna's face, but no.

There might be more I need to hear.

"You never know what will happen in the future, Jenna. If Alex is as good a man as you always thought he was then he might want to have a family with you some day."

Jenna laughs, the sound humorless and cold. "He has a wife and a baby he thinks is hers. A *good man* wouldn't walk out on that and you know it. Hell, a good man wouldn't have gotten me pregnant in the first place. You know as well as I do that I'm torturing myself for no good reason."

"You never know. Now, chin up, darling, we have work to do. Take a moment to compose yourself if you need to, but don't dally or Katie will get upset with us for not being in the house on time."

"For someone who apparently wanted a baby so badly, she sure loves passing Anna off," Jenna says bitterly. Mary doesn't reply at first. She sucks in a breath and shakes her head before speaking.

"You'll figure this out, honey, okay? Listen, tell Katie I had to pop out to the store for a moment. I doubt she's noticed that we're out of paper towels and it'll just be easier if I grab them myself. Tell her I'll be right back." Jenna doesn't respond. Mary hurries off the porch to the car and backs quickly down the driveway.

Jenna turns away from the house and stretches, rolling her head from side to side like she's trying to work out some kink there. Maybe she slept on her pillow wrong. A few months ago I would have been more than happy to massage her neck, her shoulders, her back. I would have worked out any bunches in her muscles just to take care of her.

But not now.

"Okay, you got this," Jenna mutters to herself and when I see her reaching for the door, I stand up.

"We need to talk." It's the understatement of the year but I'm still not surprised when she starts, shakes her head, and angrily jerks her chin towards the house.

"I'm supposed to be working right now. Taking care of Anna." She reaches for the door and I hurry across the porch, grabbing her wrist and pulling her hand away from the knob.

"Not yet, you're not. I told Katie you and I were going to talk this morning and she knows you'll be a bit late."

Her nostrils flare and she yanks her hand out of my grasp. I don't want to let her go, but I do, watching as she crosses her arms on her chest and stares at me.

"So talk," she says finally. "I got the impression yesterday you didn't know that your wife had hired a nanny."

"I did not. I also didn't know that our baby would be so beautiful."

She pales, just a little bit, but not enough for me to know for sure that she knows what I'm talking about.

"Anna is gorgeous. Looks just like her mom," she murmurs. There's no anger behind her words, only a question that I can tell she really wants answered.

Do you know that I'm her mom?

"Exactly like her." I know it's stupid, to want to touch Jenna right now, right here on our porch, with my wife inside somewhere, but I do, and I reach out and tuck some hair behind her ear. "Anna looks just like you, Jenna."

She steps nervously back from me. "How did you find out?"

"I saw you at the park yesterday with the stroller. It's pretty... distinctive."

She nods, her movements stiff. "That was it? That gave it away?"

"It was more than just that. Come on, Jenna. Did you honestly think I'd be able to look at you and at Anna and not figure it out??" I know my words sound angry, but actually I'm not. I'm more surprised. Surprised that Jenna thought it could go this far. Shocked that Katie didn't guess herself.

And I'm kicking myself for letting this all happen.

"I don't know." Tears fill her eyes and even though part of me would love to pull her to me so I can comfort her, I keep my hands at my sides. I don't need to hug her, don't need Katie to walk out onto the porch and see me holding her while she cries.

"What happened to Katie's baby?" It's the other question I desperately need answered and one I'm not comfortable asking my wife right now. "My real baby."

Jenna looks up, her eyes dark. "Anna is your real baby."

I sigh. "You know what I mean."

A shrug. "She lost it, I guess. And was trying to hide it from everyone."

"From me."

Jenna takes my hand and squeezes it. "Alex, I'm so sorry. You know I never would have hidden something like that from you if I were to lose our baby. But I didn't! She's healthy. She's fine. She's everything that you ever wanted — and I was the one to give her to you."

Her voice is getting higher, and louder, and I glance to the house, hoping nobody is going to walk out and hear what's being said.

So far, so good.

But I'm sure Katie will start to wonder soon what's taking so long.

"But you're not my wife, don't you see that? This isn't how it was supposed to go."

Jenna frowns. I can see her mind working a mile a minute. "Alex, does it matter? You told me your mother said you needed a baby to keep the company. I stopped taking my pill after that so you could have one. I did that for you. *For you*. Don't act now like you don't appreciate it."

"You got pregnant on purpose?" There are so many

things running through my mind that I'm going to have to sort out that right now I grab that thought, holding onto it and praying for it to make sense. "This is all because you stopped taking your pill?"

"Not all of it." Jenna shakes her head. "No, not all of it. You're a dad because I stopped taking my pill. But me stopping taking my pill didn't make Katie lose her baby. Alex, listen to me. At the end of the day Katie's gets to be a mom because of me. You're welcome."

"No." I need to get out of here. Even though I'm standing on the porch in the fresh air, I can't breathe. My chest constricts and I close my eyes, counting to ten to try to clear the thoughts I have.

Jenna is Anna's mom.

Katie lost her baby and never told me.

Wait.

"Does my wife know?" I open my eyes and stare at Jenna. How many times did the two of us curl up in bed together, whispering, laughing, enjoying each other's company? More times than I can count, and while I thought we were always on the same page, she ended up lying to me.

"About what? Anna being mine?" Jenna laughs, but the sound is dry and forced. "Yeah, right. How do you think that would have gone over with her? No way did I tell her. She has no clue."

I want to keep talking to Jenna to better understand the timeline, but just then the front door swings open and Katie is standing there, Anna in her arms, frowning as she looks at me.

33

KATIE

"This isn't going to work." I can't believe what I'm saying, but more than that, I can't believe what I just heard.

I should have known. I should have been able to look at Anna and look at Jenna and be able to tell that the two of them get along not just because Jenna is a really good nanny, but because she's her *mother*.

It's so obvious now. The answer has been literally staring me in the face. I want to scream, want to throw things, and *really* want to strangle Jenna, but I don't. I keep my fists clenched at my side and try to calm down so I don't do anything stupid that I'll regret later.

"What isn't?" Alex asks calmly as he walks over to me. There isn't a hint on his face that he knows why I'm so upset and even though part of me wants to lean against him and let him wrap his arms around me to comfort me, that's the last thing I'm going to do right now.

"This." My voice is high-pitched as I gesture, flailing, between the two of them, finally pointing at Jenna. "You. You were great, that's for sure, but you're fired."

She looks like I just slapped her. I swear, I've never seen anyone look more surprised than her right now. Before I can tell her why I'm letting her go — as if she won't know — she retaliates, her words sharp, like arrows, aimed directly at me.

"You can't fire me. You don't know how to be a mother without me." Her eyes flash and she glances at Alex like she's waiting for him to back her up. "Tell her. She wouldn't even have a baby without me. You honestly think that she can be a mother?"

"You bitch." My face flames and I raise my hand, taking a step towards her without realizing what I'm doing. "Get the hell out of my house!"

Before I can strike her, Alex is there, his hand closing around my wrist. He pulls my arm back and down to my side, his fingers warm as they press into my skin.

Squirming, I try to twist out of his grasp. "Let me go, Alex! What are you doing?"

"What are *you* doing, Katie?" His voice is low and dangerous and I stare up at him, my mouth falling open when I see the anger slashed across his face. "What are you doing, stealing a child from someone else, making me think that you had a healthy baby? What the hell were you thinking? Who the hell lies about something like that?"

"I did it for you!" How this is getting twisted around to make me the bad guy I'm not sure, but I'm not going to sit still while it happens. "This... all of this, it's for you, Alex! I tried so hard to keep my baby, and when I couldn't, I did this as the next best thing. I know how badly you want a child and to be a father and I did this for you!"

"But you didn't have to do it like this. You didn't have to do it with *her*." With his free hand he gestures at Jenna, who blinks at the two of us like she can't believe what she's hearing.

"I DID THIS FOR YOU," I repeat, even as he pulls me inside through the open front door. It already seems like a lifetime ago that I'd been standing on the other side of it, my ear pressed up against the wood, Anna asleep in her swing in the kitchen where I left her, listening to Alex and Jenna talk, hearing Jenna admit that Anna was hers.

My body doesn't feel like my own.

"I don't understand," I say, looking up at my husband as he continues to drag me through the front hall. "I thought you'd be happy. I thought you'd like what I did so that you could have a baby..."

I burst into tears.

For a moment, I don't think Alex is going to comfort me, but he slows down long enough to run a finger along my cheekbone. "Katie," he whispers, "It's okay. I know you thought you were doing the right thing. But Jenna and I need to talk this out, okay? We can figure this out. We'll figure out what we can do about this. Don't worry."

I am worried but I nod at him, gulping down air. I need to stop crying, need to think things through, but I can't. All I can do is breathe deeply, get control of myself, and trust that Alex is going to take care of this.

I should have told him everything, I should have just been honest with him from the beginning and then none of this would have happened, but I lied and now I have to rely on him to fix my mess.

I just hope he will. Ignoring the little voice in the back of my head whispering that Alex seemed way too calm about Jenna telling him Anna was hers, I finally turn to him, noticing for the first time that we are right in front of our bedroom.

When did we come up the stairs? How did he get me to walk this far with him? It feels like it was all in a dream and I give my head a little shake to try to clear it.

"Katie, I'm going to fix this," he tells me, kissing my forehead. "You have to trust me. I'm going to take care of everything, okay?"

"What are you going to do?" Reaching up, I claw at his chest, twisting his shirt in my hands. He'll be angry that he has to change or iron his shirt now before he leaves for work but I don't care.

The only thing that matters is keeping Anna.

"Trust me, okay? I'm going to take care of this." He glances over his shoulder and I look down the hall, too. He moves to one side like he's trying to keep me from seeing past him, but I see Jenna standing there.

She's frowning, but the corners of her mouth are turned up in a smirk.

I hate her.

"You'll make sure we can keep Anna? I promise you, I'll get her a birth certificate. I'll do whatever it takes to keep her, okay? Believe me, Alex, all I want is her. And you. I wouldn't have lied to you if I thought there was any other way to do this." My voice is quiet so she can't hear me, but urgent. I need to make sure Alex understands how important this is.

"I know. Just go in our room, Katie, okay? Stay there and don't come out. Give me five minutes. That's all I ask."

"Alex, no." I shake my head. "I need to know what's going on. Please."

"Five minutes, Katie, and I promise you I'll tell you everything." Another nervous glance over his shoulder.

"Please. I love you. Just do this for me. You've shown that you're willing to do anything for me, and I love that about you. Please don't stop now." There's a note of fear in his voice that I don't think I've ever heard before. Then again, never have I not trusted him to take care of me. I'm not going to start now.

Hesitating, I stare up at him. He wants me out of the way so he can talk to Jenna and even though I want to hear everything they're going to say, I can do this for him.

I trust him.

He lied to me, but I lied to him. We lied to each other, but now we both want the same thing, and I have to believe we're both going to fight to get it.

He wanted a baby? I got him one.

He needed the perfect little family? I did everything in my power to make sure he had it.

I nod at him and step back into the bedroom, my legs weak, my entire body shaking a little bit. "Five minutes," I say, and he smiles.

Alex shuts the door and I immediately lean against it, my ears straining as I listen for any scrap of their conversation.

He needs time to talk to her?

Fine. I'll give him that time.

Five minutes. I'll give him five minutes.

There are footsteps in the hall but still no voices and I strain my ears, the silence pressing down on me almost painfully. Finally, I hear something.

Something heavy scraping on the floor.

Four minutes.

The sound gets louder as it comes towards the bedroom and then stops.

Three minutes.

I'm sweating now and leaning all of my weight against the door when it shakes against me as something slams against it.

What the hell?

Stepping back, I grab the doorknob and twist it, but I can't. Something is wedged under the knob. "Alex! Alex, I want out! Let me out!"

Nothing. No answer.

He's locked me in.

34

ALEX

"Thank you," Jenna breathes, running her hands down my arm. I stiffen and turn to her, looking guiltily away from the door.

I locked my wife in our bedroom.

"That's not for you," I tell her. "It's for me, to give me time to figure things out." I take a step back from Jenna and her hands drop from my arm. "You have a hell of a lot of explaining to do. No more lies, Jenna."

She nods and opens her mouth like she's going to speak but I hold up my hand, shushing her. Katie's calling for me from the bedroom but that won't last long. She'll want to know everything that's being said and she'll fall silent to listen.

Guilt rips through me when I see the chair wedged under the doorknob, but it's tempered by the anger I feel at the situation.

She lied to me. She told me we had a baby, that our baby was perfect. She lied over and over, to everyone, after finding someone willing to give up her baby for us and taking Anna to be our own.

I still can't wrap my mind around it. I don't want to see Katie right now, much less listen to what she's going to say, and although frankly I feel the same way about Jenna, she at least has answers that I need.

"Downstairs," I say, brushing past her to the staircase. "We have a lot to talk about and you'd better explain yourself really fucking quickly."

When I look back at her the surprise on her face is obvious. I've never spoken to her like that, never once snapped at her. Our relationship was easy, fast and fun, and she's never gotten to see how I am when something isn't going the way I want it to.

"I did this for you," she says, hurrying down the stairs behind me. "You see that, don't you? This was all for you, Alex. You and Anna." We reach the bottom of the stairs and she reaches out, grabbing me by the shoulder and spinning me around. "Would you please look at me? Are you even listening to a word I'm saying?"

Her eyes are wide and sparkling with tears. "What the hell were you thinking, Jenna?" I run my hand through my hair, pushing it back from my face. "Did you think that we'd all just be one big happy family? I gave you money for Anna! I told you you'd be taken care of."

"But she needs her dad!" Jenna's not bothering to keep her voice down and I wince, hoping Katie can't hear. "She needs you, Alex, just like I do. Even though you told me we can't be together, I thought that she could still have both of her parents under one roof. Katie didn't need to know. It would be you and me and Anna and it would all be fine."

She's grabbing my arm again, her nails digging into my skin. "Don't you want to have a family, Alex? Isn't that what you need to keep the company?"

"And what, exactly, is your end game?" This is what I

need to know. "Even if we played the role of a happy little family and Katie didn't ever learn the truth, how long did you think this charade could go on?"

"It's not a charade," she cries, desperation in her voice. "This is . . . our family. You and me and Anna. That's all that matters, Alex, why can't you see that?"

"Because it's a pipe dream, Jenna, and it's never gonna happen." Groaning, I take a step back from her. She keeps holding onto me but I need space. I need to get away from her. I need to be able to breathe so I can think because right now nothing is making any sense.

"And Katie really didn't know?" Before the words are out of my mouth, Jenna is shaking her head.

"No, she was clueless. Until just now when she heard us in your office." The implication is clear — if I hadn't pushed things just now then my wife would still be in the dark about everything and Jenna would get the family she wanted, twisted as it was. "Please, Alex, I'm sure we can get her on board."

I laugh, unable to stop myself. "You honestly think she'll be okay with you, Anna's real mother, living in our house and taking care of her? Not a chance."

"Then divorce her. Marry me."

"What?" I exhale explosively. "You've got to be kidding, Jenna, that can't happen."

"Why not? People get divorced all the time. We'll wait until you get the company all signed over to you and then you can leave her and be with me. We can live here or somewhere else, it doesn't matter, and you'll have everything you wanted. So will I."

"Jenna, no, it doesn't work like that."

"Oh, but it does." She draws herself up and steps closer to me, reaching up and looping her hands around the back of my neck before lightly dragging her nails across my nape.

A shiver runs down my spine.

"You were willing to throw everything away with Katie to be with me before. Why, now that I'm promising you exactly what you want, are you not willing to take that step? We have a future together."

I don't have an answer for her.

All I know is that my wife is upstairs, locked in our bedroom, and I'm not sure how much longer I can keep her there.

35

KATIE

How could I have been so blind?

Jenna is Anna's mother.

Alex wanted to get rid of me while he talked to her.

That can only mean one thing.

He's involved with Jenna. He's got to be, and how I missed it before I don't know.

Only — I do know, if I really think about it. I missed it because I was so focused on everything else. I didn't want to think that anything might go wrong with my plan, and I was willing to tamp down my concerns and thoughts if that meant I was going to get to have the baby of my dreams.

And I got her. Now I just have to make sure I'm not going to lose her.

There's no way I can bust open the bedroom door without Alex hearing me. My only choice if I want to keep Anna for my own and get her away from Jenna, maybe even away from Alex, is obvious.

I hurry to the bedroom window and push it open.

Immediately, a breeze rushes in through the open

window, blowing my hair back from my face. The air is cool and refreshing and even though I'm scared to death of what I have to do next, it's my only option if I want to get to Anna.

Lifting one leg out the window, I pause, take a deep breath, then swing my other leg out of the window.

From here it's easy to climb down the sloped roof. I did it before, when there was a large limb that fell on the roof that Mary wouldn't get down for me, but I don't think Alex knows. He'd be upset to think of me walking around on the roof.

So many lies. So many of them coming to light.

Once I reach the gutter I turn and rest my foot on the top rung of the ladder leaning up against the roof. It annoyed me yesterday when I saw the roofing crew had left it out but now I say a little prayer of grateful thanks, grip the rungs, and slowly climb down.

Heights aren't my forte, and as soon as I step into the grass and let go of the ladder I exhale in relief. But I know I don't have time to wait.

I need to get into the house and get my baby.

I hurry around the side of the house, glancing in windows as I go. It isn't until I reach the front living room window that I see Alex and Jenna standing by the foot of the stairs.

They're standing a few inches apart and I feel a wave of nausea when I see her reach up and put her hands around the back of his neck.

But I can't tear my eyes away.

How did I not see it before? There were signs, like the emails I ignored. I just wanted so badly for Jenna to be the answer to my prayers that I missed everything.

"You have to keep moving," I mutter, then crouch down and hurry past the front window, not slowing down until I'm on the porch. The spare key is hidden under the planter where we've had it for years, its imprint in the dirt on the porch clearly visible after I pluck it up and turn to the front door.

My hand shakes but I let myself in, holding my breath as I close the door softly behind me.

Voices float down the hall towards me but they're so quiet I can't make out what either of them are saying. The only thing I know is that I'm running out of time and I need to move faster.

Carefully, to avoid any squeaky planks in the floor, I creep down the hall and tiptoe into the kitchen where Anna is still in her baby swing, fast asleep, her mouth hanging open slightly.

"Come here, baby," I whisper, bending down and picking her up. She's warm, almost sticky with the heat of sleep, and grunts a little as I hold her to my shoulder. "We're getting out of here. Mommy needs you to be quiet."

She sucks in a breath and I freeze.

"Don't cry," I say, bouncing her a little as I hurry out of the kitchen, stopping only long enough to grab the bottle I made for her earlier from the counter. "God, Anna, please don't cry." I pause in the hall, glancing right and left.

Nothing.

The voices have stopped but that doesn't mean Alex and Jenna are looking for me.

It could mean . . . God, I don't want to let my thoughts go there.

I wish I had time to get a bag or find my car keys, but I'm not willing to spend any more time in this house than is necessary. What matters to me is getting my sweet girl out of here and making sure nobody tries to take her from me.

"You're going to be just fine," I murmur to her, pressing a

kiss against her small forehead. "We just have to think what we're going to do now."

My keys are too far away to risk going to get them. Without them I can't escape this house in a car.

I'm going to have to make a run for it.

Holding Anna closer, I creep back down the hall to the front door. Every movement I make is slow, measured, so nobody sees or hears me.

This is insane. My body is screaming at me to run, to hurry out of here already, to stop moving so slowly, but I'm sure that if I move too quickly then I'm going to make a sound and then Anna will be taken from me.

Still nobody coming.

Breathing through my mouth so I can be as quiet as possible, I open the door and step outside, turning and closing it as quickly as possible. The door latches and I hesitate, sure that Alex or Jenna is about to come out after me.

I can't help feeling like this is all going to collapse at my feet.

"Anna, we're going to be okay," I tell her, crossing the porch and heading down the stairs. I feel conspicuous, like someone is going to look through the window at any moment. It isn't until I make it to the end of the driveway and off our property, Anna still quiet, that I finally feel I can relax.

Each step takes me farther and farther away from the life I thought I was going to have. I fought for that life, for Alex to love me, and giving it up feels impossible. It feels wrong.

"But I'd do anything for you," I tell Anna as I shift her weight and start down the road. Our neighborhood is nothing but giant houses perched well away from the street on beautifully landscaped lots, and although I'm half-tempted to go to a neighbor to ask for help, I'm not sure what I would say.

I'm getting a vague idea what to do. I need to get to the bank, then get out of town. It feels impossible, but I know I can do it.

With Anna.

For Anna.

"With Anna, for Anna." I say, my little mantra helping me continue to take step after step even though my mind is screaming at me that this is madness, that there's no way I'm going to be able to pull this off.

I'm so caught up in what I'm thinking and in making sure I keep moving that I don't see the car coming until it's right in front of me.

36

KATIE

The sudden appearance of the car makes my heart leap, then start beating faster. They've seen me, they had to have, but still I step to the side of the road, holding Anna closer and tighter than before, and wait for the car to pass.

It doesn't.

The car slows, then stops, the passenger window rolling down as Mary leans over to stare at me.

"Katie? What in the world? Why are you walking with Anna without her stroller?"

Mary. Mary can help me.

"Thank God," I say, stumbling over to the car and resting my hand on the open window. "Mary, I need you to get me out of here. Everything's gone wrong and I need to get out of here."

"Are you okay?" She unlocks the door and I throw it open, sliding into the front seat. Anna stirs and starts to cry.

"Shh, you're okay," I coo at her. "Please, please, Anna, you're okay."

"Katie, what's wrong?" Mary grabs my arm and I look at

her even though I want to keep looking at Anna because if I look away from her something bad might happen to her. But that's ridiculous.

She's safe in my arms.

"I need to get out of here," I say. "Please, Mary. Just drive. I need to get away from here. Alex and Jenna, they're . . ."

My throat closes and I gag on the words.

"Mary starts to drive but she's not going fast enough for me.

"Faster," I say, leaning forward like that's going to get Mary to press down harder on the gas. "Mary, we need to get out of here. This is Jenna's baby. Did you know that?" I turn to her, my eyes wide, my heart slamming in my chest, the bottle I grabbed from the counter cool in my hand.

"What?" Mary sounds shocked and I relax a little bit, sinking back in my seat. "Jenna is Anna's mom?" She's driving faster now. "That's nuts. How did you find out?"

"I overheard Jenna and Alex talking," I tell her, finally feeling better about what's happening. Mary's been with me from the beginning of this and she's not going to let something happen to me. She helped me find Anna in the first place and I don't think she'd ever look in the other direction while someone tried to take her from me.

There's just no way.

"You overheard them? What else did you hear?" She sounds worried and I glance at her, but her jaw is relaxed, her eyes steady on the road.

She's probably just worried because she feels badly for me.

"Apparently they're having an affair," I say sadly, and Mary gasps. I nod. "Yeah, I saw Jenna with her hands around the back of Alex's neck. I didn't . . . I don't know how long it's been going on." Shifting position, I turn to look at Mary. "How long have you known Jenna?"

"Oh, wow." She chews her lower lip for a moment like she's really thinking. "I met her through a mutual friend a long time ago. I told you how housekeepers and nannies all know each other, right?"

"You did."

"Yeah, well, that's it." She shrugs and pulls out of the neighborhood. "I met her through someone else I knew and got to know her better at some girls' nights."

"Did I do something stupid inviting her into my house? Am I the reason the two of them are . . .?" My voice trails off. I can't bear to finish that thought and instead turn around in my seat to make sure nobody's behind us.

The road is empty.

"You did nothing wrong," Mary tells me firmly, and the conviction in her voice makes me relax. "I'm serious, Katie, all you did was want a baby, want a family. You took care of Alex by making sure he was going to get the family he wanted so badly. Nobody would ever think that you did anything wrong, okay?"

"Okay. Thank you." Even though she's making me feel better, my head still spins. I want the loud noises in my brain to quiet down but I can't seem to make them. Anna's settled back down and I hold her close, feeling guilty that I don't have her car seat to keep her safe but knowing full well that there's no turning around now.

It isn't until Mary reaches over and touches me on the shoulder that I realize she's waiting on me to answer her.

"I'm sorry," I say, shaking my head. "Did you say something?"

"I asked what you're going to do." She gestures at Anna

and then puts both hands back on the wheel. "Do you have a plan?"

"I just have to get out of there," I tell her. "Maybe you can take me to the bank so I can get some money out of my account, and then help me get out of town. I have to do whatever it takes to keep Anna safe. You see that, don't you?"

Mary nods. My eyes are locked on her face but it's completely placid and still.

It's impossible for me to read her.

"I see that you're a wonderful mom," she tells me. "Any good mom would do whatever they had to in order to keep their daughter safe. That's all you're doing."

"Is it what *you* would do, though?" I feel uncomfortable asking her about what she would do in my position since she doesn't have kids, but I need to know. She's always so sensible. "If you were a mom, would you do this?"

"If I had a daughter, I would do everything you are. And more."

Her answer satisfies me and I relax into the seat.

"Now," she says, making a right turn, "let's get you to my house and see what we need to do next."

"Thank you," I whisper, and her hand is back on my shoulder, lightly squeezing.

"Katie, you're doing what you have to. Any good mom would kill for her daughter, remember that."

37

ALEX

I can't marry Jenna.

It's what she wants, and before, you know what? I might have considered it. But not now. I have a commitment to my wife.

Pulling my phone from my pocket, I fire off a quick email to my secretary. She needs to know I'm not going to be in the office today. This mess that Jenna and Katie have caused needs to be addressed.

Now.

"What are you doing?" Jenna grabs at my arm but I pull away from her.

I did everything I could for her to have the life she deserved. I gave her more money than the two of them would ever need, but it wasn't enough. She had to move into the fucking household and ruin everything.

"I'm fixing this," I snap at her. "Don't move. I can't deal with you getting into something you're not supposed to right now. We'll talk more later. For now, I'm going to check on Katie." Without waiting to see if she's going to stay put like I told her to, I head up the stairs, each step more difficult than the last as I get closer to where I locked my wife in the bedroom.

I know Katie. She's going to be pissed. The fact that she stopped screaming and banging on the door after I wedged the chair under the knob doesn't mean she's calmed down. No no, quite the opposite.

It means I probably need to be prepared for her to come flying out of the room in a fit of rage, claws extended, when I open the door.

"Katie?" I ask, knocking lightly on the door. "Katie, can you hear me?"

Nothing. The silent treatment? Really? I'm not in the mood. We have other things to worry about right now than her feelings being hurt, and that's how the hell we're going to get through all of this.

"Katie, I'm coming in." I carefully move the chair away from the door, my heart slamming in my chest. She wouldn't be violent, would she?

No. I know my wife and she's the gentlest person I've ever met. Katie wouldn't ever do anything to hurt me, and she especially wouldn't do anything that might put Anna in danger.

Still no answer.

I let myself into the room, moving carefully, my eyes scanning the bed, the nightstands, the dresser, the curtains, as I look for where she might be hiding.

In the closet?

"Katie, I need you to come out so the two of us can talk," I say, striding more confidently across the room in that direction. It's pretty sad if she thought she had to hide herself in here to stay safe from me, but that's obviously where she is.

Except she's not. I throw open the closet door and step

inside, growing more and more confused as I look around. It's a huge walk-in closet, one of the reasons why Katie loved this house so much, and even though it's loaded on both sides with clothes and even has a bench in the middle for her to sit while she's putting on her shoes, one thing is obvious from the moment I open the door.

Katie's not in here.

"Katie? Where the hell are you?" I ask, turning around and hurrying back into the bedroom. Dropping to my knees, I check under the bed even though she couldn't possibly be under there, could she? It isn't until I stand up and turn in a slow circle that I notice the bedroom window is open.

"Dammit, Katie!" Running to the window I push it the rest of the way open and lean out. The roof here isn't nearly as steep as it is in other places on the house, and Mary told me before that Katie climbed out of the window to get a branch off the roof. My eyes flick along it, looking for signs of my wife, then flick to the ladder.

She got out.

She's gone.

She could be with a neighbor calling the police right now.

I'm they'd love to hear how I locked her in the bedroom to talk to the nanny. Then again . . . is she stupid enough to call the police when she's been raising a child who isn't hers?

"She's gone," I cry, running from the bedroom and making my way to the top of the stairs. "Katie's gone and I don't know where she went. Jenna, we have to — Jenna?"

I stop at the top of the stairs, fear gripping my throat and making it difficult for me to breathe.

Jenna's gone too.

Swearing, I rush down the stairs, taking them as quickly

as I can, my hand skittering down the handrail to help keep my balance. As soon as I'm down, I run to the left, tearing through the living room, my eyes on the kitchen door.

That's where Anna was this morning, sleeping in a little baby swing. I'd seen her there this morning and not thought twice about the drama that she was going to cause today.

At a full run now, I throw myself against the kitchen door, not slowing down as it swings open for me, but then I skid to a stop.

The baby swing is still there, but Anna is gone.

Jenna must have her.

"Jenna!" Cupping my hands around my mouth, I yell her name. "Jenna, where the hell are you?"

Silence.

The back of my neck prickles with fear and I leave the kitchen, ready to make a circuit through the house to look for them. I'm in the living room, walking by the sofa at the front of the house, when I hear a car start and I tear open the curtains.

Jenna's backing down the driveway, her arm thrown over the passenger seat, her face turned away from me.

I need Anna.

"Not a chance, you don't," I mutter, pulling my keys from my pocket and racing to the garage. I'm going to be cutting it close and I tap the steering wheel impatiently as the garage door slowly lifts. As soon as I'm able to get out, I hit the gas, backing down the driveway as quickly as possible and pulling out into the neighborhood without slowing down.

I see Jenna's car at the end of the road, already making the first turn to work her way through the maze of streets in the neighborhood.

I know I should look for Katie. There's a voice in the back of my head telling me that I shouldn't be chasing Jenna when I don't have any idea where my wife is, but right now this isn't about Jenna, and it isn't about Katie.

It's about Anna and what having a child means for my future and Jenna has her in the car, I just know it.

I don't know how I'm going to get her back but there's no way in hell I'm going to sit idly by and watch as she takes my baby away from me.

Anna's the only person I need to make it out of this. Katie and Jenna can leave, but I need Anna to secure my future and I'm not going to stop at anything to get her back.

38

KATIE

I've never been in Mary's house. She's staff and that's all, so why would she have me over to visit?

Except she's not just staff anymore, is she? She's become a friend, someone I can trust. Mary might have started out as someone Alex and I hired to take care of the house and make our lives as easy as possible, but she became a confidante, almost like a mother to me. I've never told her that, but sitting at her kitchen table now, with a cup of tea in front of me and Jenna asleep on my lap, I don't know the last time I felt this safe and taken care of.

"I have a phone call to make. Are you going to be okay here by yourself?" Mary hesitates after she asks the question, obviously worried.

"I'm fine," I tell her, relaxing back into the seat. It's padded with a thick plastic and squeaks a little when I move. Sure, it's hopelessly out of fashion, but I can't help but feel at home here. It's been decades since I was in my grandparents' house, but I remember them having similar chairs.

"Great." She gives me a smile and then leaves the

kitchen. I hear the front door open and close and I look down at my sweet girl.

"Anna Banana," I say, stroking her head. "You are so very precious to me." She's drained the bottle I brought with me and I know I'm going to need more formula soon, but Mary was insistent we stop here for a bit and let me rest. She didn't want us to be out in town and have Alex see us at the bank or the store.

She's probably got a point.

I'm also a bit worried about what will happen if he calls the police, but then I think about how he locked me in the bedroom and I feel more confident.

Surely they wouldn't make me go back to him, right? And I'm the mother, everyone will tell them that.

I look around the kitchen to soak it all in. Mary lit some candles as soon as we walked in the door telling me that it would make it smell nice with them burning. They smell like apple pie and while I've never really liked scented candles, they do make it feel homier.

The empty soup pot on the stove is bright red, as is the pot holder tossed casually on the counter. The house couldn't be any more different than the one Alex and I live in, but I feel safe and happy here.

That's something I will have to consider for the future. What kind of a house will Anna and I want to live in when we get out of here? Will we want something small like this, maybe with a beautiful back yard? I can see getting a dog when Anna is a bit older and I'll definitely want them to be able to play outside.

As I'm fantasizing about how amazing it would be to live somewhere alone with my daughter, Mary comes back in, a smile on her face, her phone no longer in her hand. She pulls out a chair across from me and sits down, taking a sip of the tea in front of her.

"How are you holding up?"

I blink rapidly to keep from crying. It's one thing to have this amazing daydream of the life Anna and I will have together when we get out of here. It's another thing entirely to go through the steps to reach that life. It feels so real to me and yet seems so far out of reach.

"I'm exhausted," I admit, and she nods. "Thank you, Mary, for picking me up. I don't know what I would have done if you hadn't been coming up to the house right then. This is a nightmare."

"It is," she agrees. "Why don't you tell me exactly what's you're going to do?"

It feels a little silly to confess to her my daydream I was just having about the life I want to build with Anna, but why not? She's on my side and hasn't left me alone for a moment.

Except to make that phone call.

I'm curious who she called, but it's none of my business. Mary might be helping me out right now, and I really appreciate it, but she still has her own life going on. I can't except her to tell me everything about what she's doing.

"Well, okay." Exhaling hard, I snuggle Anna closer. "If Jenna is Anna's mom, I have to get out of here. She didn't want her at first, was willing to give her up, and now — what? She wants her back? I'm not sure why she would take the job in our house otherwise." I chew on my lower lip, trying and failing to put myself in Jenna's shoes.

"What about Alex?"

"What about him?" I laugh bitterly. "You didn't see the two of them together at the bottom of the stairs. I don't know how I missed it this entire time, but they're definitely together." I glance down at Anna, almost afraid to say what I overheard.

I don't want to admit the truth I just learned.

If I say it out loud, it makes it real.

"What is it, Katie? There's more to the story than what you're telling me, that much is obvious. You can tell me, okay? You can trust me."

"I know I can. You've been nothing but amazing and I really can't thank you enough for what you're doing to help me out. OK, here goes. Alex and Jenna had an affair and Anna is their daughter together." I pause, staring at my hands, letting the words hang in the air. "But how did this all happen? Why would Jenna put herself through giving up the baby only to come work at the house where she lived? Where Alex lived? It makes no sense."

Mary doesn't respond.

"I don't know," I continue. "All I know is that I need to get Anna out of here. Get her somewhere safe. I need to make sure nobody ever tries to take her from me again. She's my daughter."

"You just said she's Jenna's."

I stare at Mary. "What? Sure, Jenna gave birth to her, but she gave her up at the first possible opportunity and then freaked out and decided she needed to be around her again. Tell me how that's being a good mom."

"Hey, I'm on your side here," Mary says, holding up her hands defensively. "I'm just asking the hard questions so you really think through what you're about to get into and you don't make a mistake or something."

"Okay, I'm sorry," I say, although there's still something about this that's not sitting right with me.

I suddenly wish I had taken the extra risk to get my car keys. If I had my car, Anna I would be long gone. We could have already swung by the bank and gotten cash and would be on our way.

Shifting in my seat, I look at Mary. Her head is cocked slightly to the side, like she's listening for something.

"You told me before that a good mom will do whatever she has to for her daughter," I say, feeling more and more uncomfortable. "You must have had a great mom to think like that."

"I did," she tells me, smiling, but she's not looking at me. She's looking out the front windows, and I turn around to see what she's looking at.

Nothing exciting, not even some neighbors walking around outside. Just our car in the driveway.

"What are you looking at?" I ask. My skin feels chilled and I stand up, my chair scraping loudly against the floor. It sounds awful but I don't apologize and Mary doesn't seem to notice. "What are you looking *for*? What are you waiting for?"

I hear a car door slam but when I turn and look again I still don't see anyone in the driveway. Glancing back at Mary, I'm surprised to see her look relaxed. She still hasn't answered me.

"Mary?"

"Oh, Katie," she tells me, standing now too. She's between me and the door and I have a sudden urge to try to run past her. I could make a break for it, try to get out of the house, but the look on her face is almost daring me to make a move.

Anna wakes up and starts to cry, her wail quiet at first before it reaches a fevered pitch that makes me want to cover my ears.

"We're all just doing what's best for our daughters," Mary tells me, and then I hear the front door slam. I swallow hard, hardly daring to look away from Mary's face to see who's coming in.

Jenna.

She doesn't look surprised to see me, any more than Mary looks surprised when the nanny walks up, loops her arm around her waist, and greets her.

"Hello, Mom," Jenna says.

And the ground drops out from beneath my feet.

39

ALEX

The first thing I notice when I park on the street a block away from Jenna's car is that she goes into a house I've never seen before, but that Mary's car is right out front, in the driveway, like a beacon calling us all here. It feels strange to see where my staff lives. I've never really thought or cared about it before.

Then Jenna hurried up to the front door and let herself in like she knew where she was going and like she was sure of her welcome. Sitting in my car, I smack the steering wheel, then get out, hurrying down the road.

The second thing I notice is that she didn't have Anna with her. No small bundle held to her chest, tucked against her shoulder. I don't think she would have left her in the car while she went into Mary's house, but what do I know?

Stopping at the side of Jenna's car, I crouch, then slowly raise up a bit to peek in the windows. There are fast food wrappers on the floor, a huge styrofoam cup in the front cupholder.

No Anna.

I work my way around to the back of the car, grateful that it's a hatchback and I can see in without having to worry about popping a trunk. Terror fills me at the idea of finding little Anna wrapped up in a bag or a blanket in the back, struggling to breathe in the back of a car parked on a street I've never been to.

But the back is also empty.

So where the hell is Anna?

I look again at the house. Jenna wouldn't have come here without a good reason. I have no idea why she would come running to Mary so quickly, but she must know something I don't.

I finger my phone in my pocket, debating calling Katie, but I already know what will happen. I press the button to speed dial her anyway, not surprised when it goes straight to voicemail.

There are two people in this world who might know where my wife and baby are and they're both in the small house I'm currently staring at. I need to get moving.

Taking a deep breath, I start up the walk, moving quickly, my eyes sweeping from side to side. I feel like I'm doing something illegal, like someone is going to stop me and ask me what the hell I think I'm doing, but I need to know the truth.

Before I reach the porch, however, I hear voices.

Angry ones.

Raised.

Fighting.

Katie.

Katie's here.

I drop back down into a crouch, trying to think through what I'm going to do. I need Anna, need the security having her will offer me for my future, and there's no way I'm walking out of here without her.

But what about Katie and Jenna?

Carefully, so I can stay hidden, I work my way to the side, moving as close to the house as possible so nobody can look outside and see me. I pause directly under a window, then slowly stand up, hands gripping the windowsill. My eyes widen when I take in the scene in front of me.

Mary, with Anna in her arms, one finger pointed right at my wife, whose back is to me. Even without seeing her face, I can tell that Katie is pissed. She has one hand on her hip, the other raised like she's going to hit someone.

Her body is turned toward Mary and I can hear her yelling.

"Give her back! You never told me Jenna was your daughter!"

Mary grins at her and shakes her head, stepping away from Katie. There's a table between them with teacups and candles on it, but I doubt that will stop my wife from attacking Mary if she feels like she needs to.

I'd wager Mary feels the same.

"She's my baby," Katie cries, and there's so much angst and longing in her voice that I almost feel bad for her. "Please, Mary, you were my friend. I thought you cared for me!"

"I do," Mary says, still holding Anna to her chest. Anna's screaming now, her face purple, her hands tight little fists. "I really do, but I have to do what's best for my daughter. We talked about that."

Jenna.

Everything seems to go into slow motion. Mary mentioning Jenna makes me look to see where she is. She's off to Katie's side, and my wife turns her head toward her like she, too, had forgotten that Jenna was in the room.

Jenna's arms are over her head, a huge red pot in her hands. The look on her face is pure rage, twisted and dark, and I can't stop from crying out when I see her bring it down hard on Katie's head.

40

ALEX

I don't mean to scream.

The last thing I want is to attract attention from the neighbors, but I can't help it.

It just comes out.

I see my wife twist, see her fall, see the bit of blood smeared on the bottom of the pot Jenna swung at her. Katie didn't stand a chance at dodging the blow — Jenna moved too quickly, fueled by rage, and swung the pot at Katie like her life depended on it.

Even with the window closed I still hear the sick dull thud my wife makes when her body hits the ground. Her head turns to the side and her eyes are closed, and from here I have no way of knowing whether she's breathing or not.

Then I look up to Jenna, who isn't staring at Katie on the floor, but has raised her gaze to the window and is staring right at me.

I feel like I should run. I need to get out of here, need to do *something*, but my baby is inside that house, in Mary's arms, and I'm not leaving without her.

"Alex?" Jenna must be yelling pretty loud for me to hear her. She puts the pot down on the counter, the color draining from her face. Even from here I can see the smear of blood on the white counter and if she notices it, she doesn't move to wipe it up. Instead, she hurries to the window, close to me, and presses her hand up against the pane. "Alex? What are you doing here?"

"You left," I manage, choking out the words. "You left and I . . ."

I what?

Jenna frowns and I know I need to give her the right answer or she's going to get angry that I followed her here.

"I needed to know you were okay," I finally say, making sure I keep my eyes on her. I don't need to look past her, don't need to see Katie sprawled on the floor.

Is she dead?

It's the right answer. Jenna's face relaxes and a smile spreads across it. "I'm okay," she says, nodding vigorously, like she feels the need to convince me of what she's saying. "I'm okay, I'm okay. And so is Anna. We can be a family, Alex."

I nod, mirroring what she's doing, even though my gut is screaming at me that I'm making a huge mistake.

Does she not remember that I told her just a few minutes ago that I didn't want to be with her? Does she not remember that I chose Katie over her?

Or does she, and has she killed my wife?

"Come in," she says, taking a step back from the window. "Come in, Alex. We can be together."

"Okay," I say, but the word is a whisper. I have no idea what I'm supposed to do right now, no clue how to get out of this. Jenna is still smiling at me, her face tilted slightly to the side, the grin on her face almost unbearable.

I go around to meet her at the front door even though the last thing I want is to go into the house where my wife is sprawled on the floor. When Jenna opens the door, she has tears in her eyes.

"Alex!" She throws herself into my arms and I reflexively hug her, pulling her to me. I don't mean to, but I can't help it, my arms automatically wrap around her. "I did what you asked. Are you happy?"

"What I asked?" I shake my head. "What do you mean, Jenna? I didn't ask you to do anything to hurt Katie."

"Of course you did." She pulls back from me, surprise written all over her face like she can't quite believe what I'm saying. "You told me you couldn't be with me because you had to be with her. So I took care of her for you."

Anna cries from the other room and I turn to stare in that direction.

This is a dream. I'm going to wake up.

"Well, say something."

She's lost her mind.

"What do you want me to say?"

"How about thank you," she tells me, snuggling back up under my chin. If she hears Jenna crying, she doesn't make any movement to go to her. "You should thank me for taking care of things for you."

"Thank you," I say, the words automatic. I don't mean them, but they fall from my lips as easily as rain from the clouds.

"I did it for us, Alex."

"I know."

"We can be together now." Still holding her, I run my fingers through her hair, trailing them down her spine, my thoughts a jumble. She killed Katie ... Katie who ruined everything ... I know I should be angry at my wife, but it's difficult to do that when she's on the floor in the kitchen, blood pooling around her head.

"We can," I whisper, but I close my eyes when I say it.

We can't.

I wanted Katie, not Jenna.

Jenna took that choice from me.

But, in the end, there's only one person I really need to get the life I want.

Anna.

41

KATIE

My head hurts.

No, scratch that. It feels like my head is in a vice, like I've had people screaming into my ears for several hours, like all of the water in my body has evaporated, and like someone is banging a drum right by my ear.

My neck hurts, my face is numb from pressing into something hard and cold, and when I reach up to run my fingers along my temple, they come back sticky.

Blood.

I don't have to see it on my fingers to know that's exactly what it is. A soft groan slips from my lips but I stifle it, unsure if anyone might be close, if anyone might be listening.

Nobody comes. Nobody drops down to their knees to check on me.

From far away I hear a baby crying and I squeeze my eyes shut, wishing someone would get the kid to shut up already.

Where is the damned mother?

"Oh, shit," I mutter, finally recognizing Anna's cry. "Oh, Anna."

It all comes rushing back. I see Alex and Jenna talking, remember how I took Anna and ran, how Mary helped me, how Jenna showed up.

How something hit me and I crashed to the floor.

Planting both hands, I push myself up and am immediately so dizzy I have to lie back down. Darkness gathers at the edges of my vision and I moan, the sound escaping my lips like a whisper.

Through it all, there's a voice in the back of my head screaming that if I stay here on the floor then I'm going to lose Anna, and that simply can't happen. Even though I just want to continue to lie here forever, or at least until the darkness that's clouding my vision takes over and I can finally relax into whatever is coming next, I push myself up from the floor.

She's screaming.

And when I hear it, I get up.

"Where are you, baby?" I grab the counter to keep from falling over as I walk through the kitchen. Each step is unsteady as I put one foot in front of the other, but I have to get to Anna.

I've never been in this house before today but it's small and the rooms all connect to each other and I walk right into the dining room from the kitchen. It's obvious Mary uses this room as her living room, too. There's a TV mounted on the wall, its remote on the dining table, a few plants on one end of the table, and a small china cabinet on the other wall.

But no Anna.

Her cries are getting louder, though, I and walk into the next room.

The living room. Or rather what would be the living room if Mary didn't use the dining room for that space.

"What the hell?" I stare around me, trying to take it all in. The walls are covered with pictures, most of them of Mary and Jenna, and I feel my heart lurch when I see similarities in the two women I never noticed before. How on earth did I not pick up on the fact that they're related?

Besides the pictures of Mary and Jenna, there are ones of little Anna in the hospital right after she had been born. I walk over to them, Anna's cries fading for a moment as I lose myself in what a cute little newborn she was.

And although it's weird to see baby pictures of the child I consider mine on someone else's wall, those aren't the ones that made me stop dead in my tracks in the doorway.

It's the ones of Jenna and Alex. The selfies they obviously took in bed, laughing and snuggling.

Shaking my head, I look over a desk that's in the middle of the room. There, on the floor, is my baby girl, kicking and screaming, her eyes squeezed shut, her fists in tiny little balls of rage.

Without thinking, I rush to her, and I go to pick her up, but then I stop.

If she suddenly stops crying, Jenna and Mary are going to come here to try to figure out what's going on, and when they see me with her, they're going to take her from me. I just know it.

"I'm so sorry, baby girl," I whisper, lightly touching a finger to her forehead. She turns to face me, her mouth opening and closing, hoping for a bottle, and I feel my stomach twist. "I have to figure out how we're going to get out of here before I pick you up."

Listening for voices, I stand, and even though it kills me, I walk away from Anna. I hate leaving her there on the floor crying for me, for someone, anyone to pick her up, but I have to come up with a plan to get out of here.

Voices drift towards me and I take a few steps to the stairs leading up to the second floor before I realize that they're not coming from there. Turning and trailing my fingers along the wall to help me keep my balance, I walk towards the front of the house, finally stopping at a door that's slightly ajar.

That's where the voices are coming from.

Carefully, quietly, I push the door open a few more inches and stand in the doorway, my hands gripping the doorframe, my breathing shaky as I try to stay as silent and still as possible.

There's another set of stairs leading down to the basement. Even though I can't see what's going on down there, it doesn't really matter.

I can hear it all just fine.

42

ALEX

Mary and Jenna are struggling to get luggage down from a high shelf in the basement and even though I know I should probably make a move to help them I feel like I can't shift my feet from where they're glued to the floor.

Jenna glances over her shoulder at me. "You know I did this all for you, right?" She's out of breath, panting a little bit, and her eyes are narrowed, locked on me like lasers.

I nod, unable to respond.

"I'd do anything for you, Alex."

I nod again.

There are no words I can use to tell her how I really feel right now, how disgusted I am with her and her mother, how much I hate even being in this basement with her. At one point I thought I could have a life with her if Katie wasn't in it any longer. Now I just want Anna, just want a future with the two of us.

I know I should be screaming at Jenna, doing everything I can to get away from her, but if I'm going to save Anna, save my baby, then I need to be smarter than that.

I have to be patient. I have to wait.

Mary and Jenna finally wrestle down a large green suitcase and Jenna clutches it to her chest, triumphant, then turns to look at me again. "You're coming with me, right? I know we can't move into your house right away, and we'll have to get rid of Katie's body of course, but there's no reason why we can't be the family you've always wanted, Alex."

I wish she wouldn't say my wife's name.

Looking up at the ceiling, I try to imagine if Katie is sprawled out on the floor right above me or if she's somewhere else. I don't know the layout of this house, never even been here. When Jenna and I would get together we'd always meet up at a hotel I paid for, or in a bar.

I had no idea she lived with her mother. No idea her mother worked for us. No idea of any of it.

"I think I'd like that," I tell her, forcing some words out so she'll stop staring at me the way she is. She looks angry, like she's on a short fuse that could easily be set off. I glance away from her, staring around the rest of the basement.

Christ, it's depressing down here. No windows, no doors to the outside. The contrast between this house and my house is unbelievable. I can't imagine sweet Anna ever growing up here, ever inviting friends over to play here.

I also can't imagine her without a mother, but one is dead and the other is dangerous. I have to figure out how to get Anna away from here so it can be just the two of us.

"What are you going to do with the body?" It's only the second time Mary has spoken to me since we all came downstairs. I can still hear Anna screaming her head off upstairs, but when I'd offered to go get her earlier and comfort her, Mary had told me not to move, told me she'd see to it I never made it up the stairs if I even tried.

When I'd seen how close her hand was to a large hunting knife, I believed her.

"Me?" I croak out the word and lightly touch my chest. "What am *I* going to do with Katie's body? I'm not the one who killed her."

My sweet Katie, her eyes closed, her neck turned so painfully. She didn't deserve to die like that, all alone, so scared, without someone there to comfort her.

Even though she lied to me.

"No, but it's in your best interests to get rid of it. You're her husband. You're going to be the first suspect." Mary's voice is low, dangerous. "So you'll get rid of her and we'll be there to help run the house and take care of Anna. Then, when enough time has passed, it will only make sense for you and Jenna to grow a connection. Nobody will bat an eye when you two marry. You can have the family you always wanted."

Chills run up my spine.

"You've planned this all out."

"You pushed our timeline," Mary says, shrugging. My heart leaps into my throat as she casually fingers the knife. "So, Alex, what's the plan?"

"I'm going to move her body," I say, shocked at the words I hear coming out of my mouth. I have to keep reminding myself that the only way I'm going to have any life at all, especially one with Anna, is to make these two women believe I'm on their side.

When it's all over and done with I can figure out how to get rid of them.

For now, though, I need them to think I'm on the same page as them.

"Where?" Jenna asks breathlessly. Her lips are parted a little and her eyes are bright. "Where will you put her?"

"The back woods," I answer automatically. "I'll put her in the back woods and nobody will ever know. We'll make it look like she ran away, like she couldn't take it any longer. I can use her card, clean out one of our accounts, make it look like she disappeared."

"That was her plan anyway," Mary says casually, waving the knife towards the stairs like she's ready for me to lead the way up to the main part of the house. "So you might as well help her along with her plan. Don't worry, Alex, we won't tell anyone a thing as long as you take care of the three of us."

She smiles but it doesn't reach her eyes. When Jenna turns to look at me, too, I shiver at how similar the two of them are.

I should have seen their relationship.

I should have seen all of this coming.

Steeling myself, I walk up the stairs, moving slowly, taking my time. Each time I have to lift my foot and take another step I need to mentally prepare myself to do it.

Sighing, I reach the door and grab the handle.

Didn't we leave it open?

It doesn't matter. Nothing matters right now. The only way to have some remnant of the life I've fought so hard for is to walk through this door and do what Mary and Jenna want me to.

There's only one problem.

The door's locked.

43

KATIE

I hear what Alex says about burying me in the back woods and those words swirl around me as I lean in the doorframe, my head spinning, my knees so weak they feel like they're going to give out.

". . . like she ran away, like she couldn't take it any longer. I can use her card, clean out one of our accounts, make it look like she disappeared." The words float up to me and I can't help the small gasp I make, but it's quiet enough that nobody in the basement hears me.

Alex is going to kill me.

I know what I have to do.

My heart slams hard in my chest as I shut the door to the basement, holding the handle carefully so that it doesn't make a loud noise. Even though it's the smart thing to do, the *only* thing to do, I hold my breath as I lock the door. There's another latch close to the top of the door — a child safety latch — and I have to stand on my tiptoes to reach it.

But I manage to get to it and I throw it, locking my husband, my nanny, and my housekeeper in the basement.

A small voice in the back of my head is telling me this is wrong, but I know that's not true. It's self-defense.

If I'm going to have Anna as my child and keep her safe then I have to do this. I'm her mother.

Mothers do whatever is necessary to keep their daughters safe. Isn't that what Mary told me?

"Let's see how you like being locked in somewhere," I mutter, but the words don't bring me any joy. I feel weighed down and heavy as I walk back to Anna, doing my best to move as quickly as possible now.

I'm not sure how much time I have to play with. I don't know if there's another way out of the basement, if they're going to check the door and then climb out of a basement window to run around to the front of the house and surprise me at the door.

The important thing is to get Anna. I push myself to go even faster, and in a moment I'm crouched next to her, scooping her up, resting for a second or two with one hand braced on the floor so I don't pass out.

My vision is fading in and out but I'll power through to keep my little girl safe.

How I didn't die on the kitchen floor is beyond me, but I'm alive, and that's all that matters.

"Come on, baby girl," I whisper. She's still screaming for food but I don't have anything with me right now. I'm going to have to get to my house to get her a bottle, which means putting up with her screaming a bit longer.

I can do that.

I'm walking through the kitchen, Anna pressed against my chest, when I hear it.

Someone slamming against a door.

"Katie!" I hear my name, then a string of words, but they're difficult to make out and I can't tell what's being said.

I know who it is, though.

Alex.

"What are we going to do?" My head starts to swim and I lean against the counter for a moment to try to steady myself so I can think. Anna keeps screaming, the sound right in my ear. Everything around me is crystal clear, the candle flames flickering on the table, the bright smear of my blood on the floor. For a moment, I lose myself in the beauty of the flames. Then I frown.

Those wicks should have been trimmed before the candles were lit. They're too high, too hot. It's dangerous. I'd never allow candles like that anywhere near my little girl. Anger flows through me to think Mary believed they were okay, that Anna would be safe around them.

Then it hits me.

I'll burn the place down.

I should feel regret, should feel *something* at the thought of lighting a house with three people in it on fire to get away with Anna, but I don't. The only thing I feel when I reach for a candle, my hand closing around the glass holder, is resolution.

"Let's say goodbye to Daddy," I whisper to Jenna, then walk with the candle into the dining room. The drapes on the window reach the floor and I put the candle down next to them and tip it over, watching as the flames dance and lick their way up the fabric. It only takes a moment for the curtains to be completely engulfed in fire, the sound loud, the heat already pouring off of them.

That was fast.

I'm moving with renewed purpose now and I hurry back into the kitchen and grab the other candle. The jar is hot and it burns my fingers a little but I ignore the pain as I walk to the basement door. All I have to do is following the banging. All I have to do is listen for my husband calling my name, his voice raw with fear, then crouch down and put the candle on its side by the door.

For a moment, I don't think it's going to work. I'm sure that the wood will be too thick, too new, too *something* and that my plan will fail spectacularly, but eventually the flame catches the wood, licking up it, the bottom edge of the door quickly glowing red.

"Goodbye, Alex," I whisper, even though I know he can't hear me over his own screams.

I wonder how long it will take for the smoke to curl under the door. I wonder if he'll feel the heat through the door first or if he'll smell the smoke. Part of me would love to stick around and find out myself, but I need to save Anna.

I did this all for her, after all.

Standing, I stumble away from the door. Turning once, I look behind me and see the bright flames in the dining room. They've spread from the curtains to the walls and are dancing around the room, poking long fingers of flame into both the living room and the kitchen.

In just a few minutes, the house will be completely engulfed and I have to make sure Anna and I aren't anywhere near it.

She's still screaming as I take her outside onto the porch, holding her close so I don't accidentally drop her. I make sure to shut the front door behind me. On the porch I pause, wondering for a moment how I'm going to get home.

I'm sure I look a wreck, but there aren't any neighbors outside to see me.

I'll walk.

My legs are heavy and all I want to do is sleep, but Anna's screaming will keep me up. I'll make it home with her because I don't have any other choice. If I want to be a mom — want to be Anna's mom — and I want to protect her, then I have to make it home.

I stumble away from the house, pure adrenaline and Anna's screams the only things keeping me going.

I don't look back.

44

EPILOGUE

It was huge news when Alexander Stanfield, the head of Stanfield Investments, was trapped in a house fire and killed. Everyone was shocked, surprised, and had more questions than answers.

Well, everyone but me.

Grabbing the newspaper from the box, I wave at the neighbor across the street. Walter. He probably has thirty years on me and waves pleasantly, watching me as I walk back into the house. Everyone watches me now, like they're waiting to see what I'm going to do without Alex.

And the answer? *Nothing.*

Right now Anna and I are going to stay right here in this house, where we belong. I'm not going to move, not when I have no reason to. A lot of information has come to light after Alex's death, some of it not so great.

Like the fact that he needed an heir to keep the company in his name, but then again I knew that. And as soon as she met Anna, Alex's mother gladly resigned as CEO and handed over the reins to him. Last I heard, she was living it up in Europe somewhere.

But what neither he nor I knew was that, in the event of his death, the company passed on to me, just as it passed to his mother when his father died. Working outside of the house isn't something I've ever wanted to do, and I don't know the first thing about investing anyway, but investors from all over the country were thrilled to line up for the opportunity to move to Tennessee and take over the running of the business.

Now all Anna and I have to do is sit back and collect the checks as they roll in.

It's a lot like being married to Alex, except I don't have events I have to go to with him and I don't need to worry about whether or not I'm going to be able to give him the child he wants. There's zero pressure, and since I don't have to work outside the home, there's no need to hire a nanny.

I enjoy being a mom. Besides, how in the world would I ever trust a nanny again?

I have a team of cleaners that comes in twice a week, and security who keep an eye on the place 24/7.

Paranoid? Sure, but I have Anna to protect.

Back inside the house I lock the front door, then scoop her up from the sofa, settling down next to her with the newspaper spread on my lap. "Let's see what kind of things the press is saying about the fire now," I murmur, tracing her cheek with my finger. "By the time you grow up, you won't have to hear any of this, don't worry."

Unfolding the paper, I toss the sports and comics to one side, then flick my wrist to smooth out the front page. The fire was the top story for the longest time, dominating the headlines everywhere I looked. Nobody could get enough of the tragic story of Alex Stanfield, cut down in the prime of life, burned to death at his housekeeper's home.

It didn't make sense to anyone, and I didn't chip in any

info to make it make sense to the police. His car was there, the fire was ruled — well, that verdict is still out, but I'm not worried. I wasn't anywhere near there. Nobody saw me.

At least, nobody's come forward to say that they have. The fear I had about that, the fear of the doorbell ringing or someone calling me, has diminished day by day. If anyone saw me there at the house they would surely have reached out to me by now, or called the cops, or something.

Something.

"That headline," I say, pushing that fear back to the back of my mind and ignoring the way it festers there as I skim the first paragraph, "*Two bodies found in the wreckage of the Stanfield housekeeper's home.*" I pause and look over at my daughter. "That's a little wordy for a headline, don't you think, Anna Banana?" I ask.

Then it hits me.

I said the word and glossed right over it.

"Two?" I whisper, setting Anna to my side so I can smooth out the paper on my lap and get a better look at it. "Only *two* bodies found?"

My pulse speeds up and I feel my palms start to sweat. I wipe them on my jeans, then pick the paper back up, holding it closer to my face now so I can get a better look at the words. I need to make sure I'm not seeing things.

"The blaze last month is still under investigation, but new details have been released that don't do anything to shed new light and understanding on what occurred," I say, reaching out to rest one hand on Anna's stomach. She's been trying to roll a lot recently and the last thing I want is for her to accidentally fall off the sofa while I'm trying to get my brain to comprehend what I'm reading.

"Detectives and the Fire Marshall are still working together to try to determine the cause of the blaze, which appears to have started in two different places inside the house, leading to speculation that it may not have been accidental. The release of this new information that there was an additional body in the basement besides the one already identified as the investor Alexander Stanfield creates more questions than answers."

If this were a movie then I'd be reaching for the remote to turn it off so I could catch my breath, but this is real life and the only way to get through to the end is to keep reading.

"The investigation is ongoing as detectives try to determine the identity of the second body in the basement. The first thought is that it belongs to Mary Waters, the Stanfields' housekeeper, and the owner of the house. Anyone with any information is encouraged to call Detective Hardy."

The article goes on for paragraphs but I put the paper down, my hands shaking.

Two bodies.

Two.

I locked three people in the basement. I tried to murder three people to stop them from taking my sweet Anna from me. I thought that I succeeded, that I protected her, that I fixed it so that nobody would be able to hurt her or threaten her again, but I was wrong.

Someone made it out alive.

ALSO BY EMILY SHINER

The Caretaker

The Promise

Not My Sister's Keeper

The Secret Wife

She Knew He Lied

The Liar House

The Good Teacher

The Silent Prodigy

The Bad Nanny

Made in the USA
Monee, IL
06 October 2022